"You're not the kind of man I want my son to look up to," Sharon said. "You're a drifter, a wanderer, and when spring comes you'll be on your way again."

"What kind of a man do you want to set an example for your son, that tight-faced banker I've seen you with?" Marc asked, his gaze hot.

"Why not? He's a good man, kind, steady, settled. He's . . ." *Safe*, she was about to say.

"Dull? Boring?"

She looked away. So what if what she wanted was someone who couldn't hurt her, as her first husband had. Wasn't security what mattered?

"Do you want dull, Sharon? Do you want boring? Or do you want this?" Marc said, his voice a low growl as he pulled her into his arms, and a wild excitement flared through her. "I can see it in your eyes, how you want me. I can feel it in the tension of your body whenever I stand close to you. I can hear it in your breathing, right now. You want me, and I want you too. Someday, you'll admit it."

"No!" She moaned, and when his mouth came slowly toward hers she did not turn her head away. Mesmerized, she felt his lips brush hers, until need and curiosity overcame caution, and her lips reveled in the taste and feel of this man who made her feel alive again. . . .

WHAT ARE *LOVESWEPT* ROMANCES?

They are stories of true romance and touching emotion. We believe those two very important ingredients are constants in our highly sensual and very believable stories in the *LOVESWEPT* line. Our goal is to give you, the reader, stories of consistently high quality that may sometimes make you laugh, sometimes make you cry, but are always fresh and creative and contain many delightful surprises within their pages.

Most romance fans read an enormous number of books. Those they truly love, they keep. Others may be traded with friends and soon forgotten. We hope that each *LOVESWEPT* romance will be a treasure—a "keeper." We will always try to publish

LOVE STORIES YOU'LL NEVER FORGET
BY AUTHORS YOU'LL ALWAYS REMEMBER

The Editors

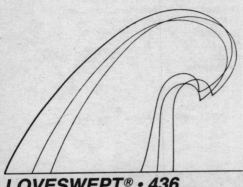

LOVESWEPT® • 436

Judy Gill
Moonlight Man

 BANTAM BOOKS
NEW YORK • TORONTO • LONDON • SYDNEY • AUCKLAND

MOONLIGHT MAN

A Bantam Book / November 1990

LOVESWEPT® and the wave device are registered
trademarks of Bantam Books, a division of
Bantam Doubleday Dell Publishing Group, Inc.
Registered in U.S. Patent
and Trademark Office and elsewhere.

If you would be interested in receiving protective vinyl
covers for your Loveswept books, please write to this
address for information:

Loveswept
Bantam Books
P. O. Box 985
Hicksville, NY 11802

ISBN 0-553-44067-5

Published simultaneously in the United States and Canada

Bantam Books are published by Bantam Books, a division
of Bantam Doubleday Dell Publishing Group, Inc. Its trademark, consisting of the words "Bantam Books" and the
portrayal of a rooster, is Registered in U.S. Patent and
Trademark Office and in other countries. Marca Regis-
trada. Bantam Books, 666 Fifth Avenue, New York, New
York 10103.

PRINTED IN THE UNITED STATES OF AMERICA

OPM   0 9 8 7 6 5 4 3 2 1

One

The moon was high in the night sky. The man walked slowly up through the woods along a path he saw only dimly. No matter, he had climbed that same hill many times within the past several months. His feet knew it even though he couldn't see it well. Coming to his favorite spot, he sat on the flat surface of a cold rock, just where a break in the leafless trees gave him a fine view of the moon and its silver reflection on the ocean waters far below.

As he sat, he began to speak as if his listener were right beside him. In a way, for sixteen years she had been, but for the past six, he could never be certain that she heard him.

"Simone, I have to tell you about someone, someone I believe is the only woman other than you I can care for. In many ways, I already do. I like the way she looks. She has sleek black hair that hangs like a bell around a tiny, delicate face, and jet-black eyes that flare with light when she's annoyed." He paused, smiled to himself, and then went on. "Where I'm concerned, unfortunately, she's mostly annoyed, yet I love to see her eyes flash anyway. She moves like a skater, gliding. I could watch her for hours. Someday I want to dance with her. Whenever I have an opportunity to be close to her, the scent of her makes me dizzy. Her voice . . . she has the most beautiful speaking voice, like a fine-tuned instrument playing a melody. Her name is Sharon, Simone, and she has two children, a ten-year-old boy and a six-year-old girl. Our family would have been exactly the same if the world hadn't caved in on us when it did. I met her son Jason first, and then I met Sharon. And though she doesn't like me or want to know me, I think she is simply doing what I did for so many of those years after I lost you. She's running, because she's afraid to love again. She will, though. I recognize the way she looks at me, half fascinated, half afraid, and angry with me for making her feel that way. Probably angry with me simply for making her feel.

"Don't think that this means I intend to forget you or Jean-Pierre or the little one who might have been our daughter. You will all live on in my heart forever. But six years is too long for a man to be alone without a family, without a love. I'll play one more song for you, the one I played on our wedding night." His voice fell to a whisper. "It will be my final good-bye to you, Simone. It's time for me to move on again, not to another town, another country, but into a future. Right here."

For a moment the man sat there, his head bowed, then he stood and resumed walking as he put his old, worn harmonica to his mouth and began playing softly. As he walked aimlessly across the top of a nearly treeless hill, he played louder, hoping the song was winging its way upward to where his dead wife and children might hear it and rejoice with him in his new-found hope for tomorrow.

Yet it was from far below that an answer came in the form of a female voice crying, "Help! Help! We're down here! Help!"

As he heard that faint voice, Marc Duval froze where he stood. "Where are you?" he shouted, and when the woman replied that they were in a cavern nearly under his feet, he knew. His heart swelled, and a smile grew broad across his thickly bearded face. "Are you Jeanie Leslie?" he called, and when the answer came back, he breathed a silent thank-you to Simone for giving him this chance, for surely she had been the one to lead him this way, offering him her blessing to go on and live his life.

Because how could Sharon Leslie possibly resist him now? He had found her sister, who had been missing and feared dead for the past ten days!

"Jason Murcady!" Sharon stood, hands on her hips, glaring down at her ten-year-old son. She spoke angrily but quietly; she didn't want her guests to know that the sister of the bride was furious with one of her children. "When I said that you and Roxanne could each invite one friend to Aunt Jeanie and Uncle Max's wedding, I did not mean that man! I meant one of your school friends, and you know it! It was so you could have someone special of your own age to talk to among all these adults."

"But Mom, Marc is special. And I did tell you I was inviting him."

"You know as well as I do that when you said Marc, I assumed you meant Mark Simpson. That's twice you've pulled that one on me, Jason. It won't happen again. I'm onto you now."

"But Mom—"

"But nothing! You know how I feel about Marc Duval."

"Why don't you like him, Mom?"

Sharon hesitated, biting the inside of her lip. She couldn't tell her son that she found the way Marc Duval looked at her distinctly unsettling, or that her own response to those looks was just as disturbing. "Jason, I can't explain it. It's just . . . just something I can't explain, but it's true. I wish he wasn't here."

Lifting her troubled gaze from her son's rebellious face, Sharon transferred it across the room to the man who stood talking, laughing, gesturing, looking to all the world as if he belonged in her living room, when the fact of the matter was he belonged in no one's living room. The man was a drifter, without visible means of support. He lived in a battered old camper, for heaven's sake—a battered old camper parked not ten feet from the wall of her patio. Every time she saw him, her hackles rose, in spite of what he had done for her family. Now, she watched as he put an arm around her soon-to-be brother-in-law's shoulder and laughed at something Max said, then leaned over and ducked under the brim of the incredible hat worn by Freda Coin, Max's research assistant. Marc Duval kissed the elderly woman's cheek and said something that raised a laugh from the crowd around him.

Dammit, he fit in all too well! Normally clad in tight jeans and flannel shirts with his bushy beard and overlong hair every-which-way, this afternoon he was dressed in a dark suit that she was certain was cashmere, and a pale pink shirt with a burgundy and blue striped pure silk tie. He'd had his beard trimmed and his hair cut, but it was still longer than she thought fashionable. Only on him it looked good.

She found herself furious that he'd cleaned up so nicely. She would have preferred he remain the drifter she knew him to be and drift away on the next outgoing tide.

Then, as if sensing her stare, he turned his head toward her. With a smile, he broke free of the group and crossed the room, moving in her direction, she thought with whimsy that angered her even further, like a well-dressed mountain lion. Her heart hammered high in her chest as Marc Duval approached, his topaz eyes fixed on her face. He was giving her that . . . *look* again, that hungry, seeking look that she knew she was responding to with one of her own, as hard as she tried to stop it.

"Hi, Jase," he said, giving her son a quick squeeze, never taking his gaze from Sharon's face. He smiled at her. "Ms. Leslie. It was good of you to invite me," he said, and extended his hand.

She had to take it. Politeness dictated that she do so. His hand was huge and engulfed her own, making her feel hot and bothered, the way Marc Duval always made her feel whenever he came into the library where she worked, or she saw him in the supermarket or the post office or the backyard of the Harding place over her patio wall.

She snatched her hand free and locked it with her other one behind her back as she struggled against the tumultuous feelings he aroused in her.

"Not at all, Mr. Duval," she said stiffly. "I'm sure if Jason hadn't asked that you be given an invitation, my sister would have. We are all very grateful to you for having found her and Max."

Liar, he said silently, trying hard not to laugh. He knew she was grateful that her sister was safe, but he also knew that she wished it had been anybody but he who had been instrumental in finding her.

But it was Christmas Eve and her sister's wedding day. And she had invited him. Surely she had to feel some form of human kindness toward him? If she did, it was hardly reflected in the cool smile with which she introduced him to a couple who had just arrived. As she stood chatting with the others, he watched her unobtrusively, the changing expressions, her quick smile, her laughing eyes. From the moment he'd first seen her from his camper next door, he'd been captivated. But she'd never stood still long enough for him to have a chance to introduce himself. In fact, it had soon become obvious that she avoided her patio whenever he was in residence next door. He'd met her kids and had come to like them very quickly, as he did most children. But their beautiful mother had remained intriguingly elusive.

Now, as the conversation ebbed and flowed without the necessity of his adding to it beyond an interested nod or smile, he remembered that first time he'd spoken to her, and how her instant animosity had set him back on his heels. *She knows! How in hell does she know?* The knowledge and the question had slammed into him with immediate and shocking impact. Yet, it seemed impossible that his past had followed him so far. He'd changed his name, changed his appearance, stopped practicing his profession, even moved across the country. He'd been shattered to think the only woman he'd shown an interest in since losing Simone knew his terrible story and loathed him in spite of the findings of the court.

Later he'd realized that she didn't know, that the name Marc Duval meant nothing more to her than the name Sharon Murcady had to him. He'd assumed she had the same surname as her children, but when he called her by it, her obsidian eyes had flared, and she'd said stiffly, "Leslie. My name is Sharon Leslie."

He remembered how his jaw had dropped. "Of course!" he'd said. "I knew when I first saw you on your patio that you looked familiar. I have one of your tapes, Ms. Leslie, one with your picture on it. It's wonderful. Music is one of my greatest pleasures in life."

"How nice for you," she'd said, and turned deliberately to the next customer in the library. He'd been forced to move on. Every attempt he'd made to get to know her, to develop some kind of relationship with her, had been met by the wall she'd erected between them. But this night he intended to knock that wall flat. Or at least kick down a brick or two. If only he could figure out how.

"You have a lovely home, Ms. Leslie," he said when the other people stepped away.

"Thank you." Her response was light, even though she wished with all her might that he, too, would go and talk to someone else.

"It's similar in design to mine, although somewhat larger," Marc said, watching the constantly changing expressions in her eyes. "I understand that our two properties used to be one and that mine was the guest house."

Her eyes flared. "Yours?" He was pretty proprietorial for a man who rented a bit of concrete on which to park his camper!

"I've bought the Harding place, you know."

She was silent for several seconds, looking at him in frank dismay. Since old Dr. Harding had died, his widow had rented the place to summer visitors. She'd wondered why Mrs. Harding hadn't rented it to someone else, since Marc clearly wasn't using the house. Until recently, he hadn't even been there much, just enough to drive her up the wall and make Jason glow with happiness. When Duval was gone, the boy moped. When he was there, however, *she* lived on edge all the time. It was those damned discerning eyes of his that made her uncomfortable. He made something deep inside her itch unbearably, and she was sure he not only knew it but did it deliberately.

"No. I didn't know. I thought you'd be moving on again."

"And perhaps I will. I rented for a few months to see how I fit into the area before I committed myself, but I find I like it here. However, at least for the winter, I'm moving out of the camper and into the house. I thought I'd do that tomorrow."

"I hope you'll be very . . . comfortable," she said in a tone that suggested she hoped the roof would cave in on him soon. She lifted her small chin upward and glanced toward the entry, where Max's brother Rolph had just opened the door. "You'll excuse me, I'm sure. I see the minister has arrived. I must go and greet him."

Head tilted high, she walked away, shining bell of hair swinging just above the shoulders of her gold velvet gown, the white of the dress's fur trim making her hair look even blacker. Marc sighed. She was so beautiful that it made him ache to look at her. *One day,* he promised himself, *one day soon, the flashes of disdain in those obsidian eyes are going to turn to flames of passion. For me.*

Jason returned just then, and he put an affectionate hand on the boy's neatly brushed hair. "Didn't you tell me you were going to be an usher? Maybe you could show me to my seat. It looks like there's a wedding about to take place."

"Are you two all ready?" Sharon asked as she poked her head into her sister's room. Her little daughter looked like a porcelain doll in her gold velvet gown that was a replica of her own dress. Sharon beamed at her, then stared at her sister who stood before the mirror, a look of consternation on her face.

"My hair!" Jeanie wailed, poking another pin into the French roll at the back of her head, tightening one of the antique combs at the sides.

"Your hair is beautiful," Sharon said, readjusting the little circlet of gold tinsel Jeanie had chosen for a headdress, claiming that she wouldn't wear a veil, that she was no blushing virgin and wanted to go to Max with her eyes wide open, her vision completely unobscured. "Now turn around and let me see you."

Jeanie turned slowly, showing off the heavy, creamy-white velvet gown. It had a low neckline trimmed with golden fur which circled up and over her shoulders, then followed the open vee down her back, revealing a smooth expanse of bare skin. It fell in elegant folds from its tightly fitted bodice to where the golden fur around the hem just brushed the tops of her shoes.

"Is Max here?" Her voice shook. Her gray eyes looked slightly wild.

"Of course he's here, silly. Where did you think he might be, Timbuktu?"

"I'm scared, Sharon."

Sharon gave her little sister, who stood six inches taller than she, a hug. "I know, baby, but it'll be all right the moment you come down those stairs and see Max waiting for you. Then, you won't be scared ever again," she promised with deep conviction.

Jeanie stared at her. How could Sharon have such total faith that good things were bound to happen? She was a wonderful woman, this sister of hers. Bending, she kissed Sharon's cheek. "Thank you," she said. "I love you."

"I know, babe. Love you too." Then, turning to her daughter, Sharon said, "Roxy, remember how we practiced it?" Quickly, she went through the steps of what was to happen, then, with a quick flick to straighten her daughter's already perfectly aligned dress, Sharon left, holding up the skirt of her own gown as she ran back down the hall. At the top of the stairs she paused, descending at a decorous pace.

She smiled at the assembled guests in her living room and concentrated on not meeting Marc Duval's hot stare. As she took her stool by her harp, she spread her skirts around her and lifted her hands, feeling the golden bangles her sister had insisted she wear slide toward her elbow, tinkling as they went. *Please*, she prayed silently, *let me do this right for Jeanie.*

She began playing the "Wedding March," her fingers whispering over the strings, finding their way almost without her guidance.

* * *

Max stood rooted, watching his Christmas angel descend the stairs. Her hair was perfect, not a wisp out of place. Her little golden crown of tinsel glittered in the lights. Reaching behind him, he lifted her bridal bouquet and placed it in her arms. The gray satin of her eyes silvered over with tears for just an instant as she stared in awe at the huge armful of golden daffodils he had given her, then lifted her face to his with a smile that nearly stopped his heart. "Hi," she whispered, stepping from the last stair. "Have you been waiting long?"

He reached out and flicked free a few little kinks of hair so they sprang out and caught the light around her face. "Only forever," he said, and took her arm, linking it through his, seeing the gleam of a single gold bangle on her wrist. *Something old.* With a smile, he stepped forward with his bride, leading her to their welcome fate.

"It was a beautiful wedding, Sharon," Zinnie said as she sat down, kicked off her shoes, and put her feet on the coffee table. Then, with a guilty start, she set them on the floor again.

"Oh, for heaven's sake, go ahead," Sharon said, leaning back, kicking off her own shoes, and putting up her feet. "That's what coffee tables are for in my house." She took a long drink from her glass of soda water, sighed, and looked at the children's stockings she and Max's mother had just finished stuffing and hanging from the mantel. "I'm beat!"

"And so you should be. You did your sister proud," Zinnie congratulated her. "A Christmas Eve wedding was a lot of work, but you came through like a trouper. And I just know those two are going to be as happy as Harry and I have been all these years." She picked up her glass and sipped, looking at Sharon over the rim. "Now tell me, since you caught that whole whack of daffodils right smack in the face, who's the next groom in this family?"

Sharon loved the way she and her children had been automatically included in Jeanie's new family. What she didn't love was the way Zinnie's words brought a startling image to her mind, an image of a golden-haired, bearded man with shoulders no drifter should have. He had no more business infiltrating her secret thoughts than he did coming into her living room.

"Don't look to me for an answer," she said quickly, and forced a laugh. "My little sister threatened that she'd get me, even with her back turned, and if your friend Marian hadn't ducked when she did, I wouldn't have caught that bouquet. I'm beginning to suspect there was some kind of conspiracy."

"Oh, pooh! Marian's just as bad as you are. She ducked because she doesn't want to be the next bride either. Her family has lived next door to us since she was a toddler. She followed my boys everywhere. For a while she thought she was a little boy, I'm sure, and since she grew up, she's driven her mother to despair. There are literally dozens of men after her, but she can't see them for apples. Don't tell me you're the same. I understand you've been alone for three years now."

More than that. Much more, Sharon could have said but did not. Instead, for reasons she didn't understand but which she suspected had a lot to do with that mental image she couldn't quite dispel, she shrugged and said, "I am seeing someone, but it's still a very casual relationship. He's a banker. You'd have met him today, but he's away." She shocked herself with the lie. She doubted very much that she'd have invited Lorne Cantrell to the wedding even if he'd been in town. It just seemed . . . expedient, somehow, to drag him into the conversation. He *was* the only man she'd dated for a long time.

"You're fond of this man?"

Sharon shrugged, feeling uncomfortable. "Yes. I guess so. I mean, of course. He's very . . . nice. He's kind, gentle, and well bred." Then she frowned. It sounded as if she were discussing a dog she'd seen for sale. "Why do you ask?"

Zinnie smiled. "Your face doesn't exactly light up when you speak of him. So I wondered."

"Maybe it's not that kind of relationship. Yet."

"Of course." Zinnie patted her hand. "But tell me more about him. If you had to describe him in a word, how would you do it?"

She looked at Zinnie. What an odd question. After a moment's thought, she said, "I guess I'd say quiet."

Zinnie shook her head, her salt-and-pepper hair dancing around her face. "Quiet? Funny, I'd have thought at your age you'd be looking for 'exciting,' rather than 'quiet.' "

"My age? I'm thirty-seven, Zinnie. I've been married." Her face took on a pensive, unhappy cast. "I've had 'excitement.' "

"Thirty-seven is still very young, my dear, but it's your business, of course. Now tell me, who is that utterly gorgeous golden panther of a man whom Jason kept in tow all evening? The one who followed you with his eyes."

Sharon pulled a wry face. Trust Zinnie to spot the way the man looked at her. "His name is Marc Duval."

"Oh!" Zinnie's bright blue eyes sparkled. "Yes. Of course. He's the one who found Jeanie and Max in that cave. I remember meeting him the day they were rescued, and naturally we wrote him a thank-you letter. But that day he'd been dressed in grimy jeans and a plaid flannel shirt with a hunting vest over it. He certainly didn't look like he did tonight, all sophisticated elegance—suave, debonair, perfect manners, and that delicious little hint of a French accent! He's a honey, all right. Charm right up to his beautiful eyes. They're more golden than brown. Did you notice?"

Did I notice? Only every time I've seen him. Only far too much! But Sharon was saved from having to answer as Zinnie went on:

"Where's he from? What do you know about him?"

"Not much, but what I do know I don't like. He moved onto the grounds of the old Harding place next door last summer and lives in a disreputable camper, which he parked right next to my patio wall. You must have seen it out there. Naturally, we met, or at least developed a nodding acquaintance. I didn't learn his name until he came into the library one day to borrow some books. He has Jase completely captivated and begging me for guitar lessons now. Lessons from the great Duval, of course," she added, her tone making it clear just how she felt about the situation.

Zinnie raised her brows. "Well? That's a problem?"

Sharon sighed. "I don't want Jason to have anything to do with"—she nearly said "him," but changed it at the last moment—"music. I want him to be just a normal, happy little boy. I do not want him to grow up to be a musician. And Marc

Duval keeps encouraging him. Why, that man is the reason Jason, and then Jeanie and Max, got lost in the first place," she added indignantly.

"Every night the man plays one instrument or another; his harmonica, guitar, flute, whatever, and Jason loves to hear him. When he told me he was spending the night with a friend, what he intended to do instead was sneak onto the porch swing to listen to him play. So he lied to me about where he was going and to make it look good went off down the trail and spotted that rabbit. The rest is history."

She sighed unhappily. "It's my fault, I know. For his first seven years, Jason was exposed to music daily. He misses it. He even told me so, but I didn't want to hear him."

She sighed again, and there was almost a sob in her voice. "I don't want to hear Marc Duval's music either, but I do. It was awful in the summer. I couldn't sit outside because he was always playing something. And now . . . my Lord! I almost forgot! He told me he's bought the house and is moving in. And I've been hoping he'd be moving on!"

Zinnie touched Sharon's hand. "So why don't you play for Jason if he wants to hear music so badly?" she asked gently. "It doesn't mean he has to grow up to be a musician. But how can it hurt for him to have an appreciation of it? And you're good, Sharon. Incredible. Today, you created a kind of magic with that harp of yours I've rarely heard. Your 'Ode to Joy' at the end of the ceremony moved me to tears."

Sharon gave Zinnie a quick smile. "You," she accused, "were in tears from the moment Roxy tripped and Harry picked her up. I think half the guests were afraid that you hated the thought of losing your son to my sister."

"Weddings always make me cry," said Zinnie. "But never one like that. It was the most beautiful and poignant ceremony I've witnessed, all the more so because the bride and groom are so lucky to be alive, and we are so lucky to have them." She stood, yawned, and stretched. She was ready for bed.

"Yes. I know."

"So be nice to your Mr. Duval. Remember, we do have him to thank."

"Yes," Sharon said, getting to her feet. "Good night, Zinnie. Sleep well."

Sharon paced around the house, still too keyed up to go to bed. In the darkened kitchen, she glanced out the window. Duval's camper showed no lights. Often it did, far into the night, as if he slept as poorly as she did. She wished Zinnie hadn't left her thinking about the man. She knew what they all owed Marc Duval. She'd known it now for nearly two months, and it didn't make it any easier to deal with her jumbled feelings toward him.

She left the kitchen, hoping to leave the thoughts of him behind. The living room still smelled of the cigarettes some of the guests had smoked, and her harp stood there, calling, calling, begging her to come back to it.

"No!" she whispered, and grabbed a heavy jacket from a hook near the back door. As if the opening of her door had been a signal, the music came, soft and haunting and infinitely sad. *Silent Night . . . Holy Night.* He played his harmonica quietly, but all was not calm, not in Sharon's heart. It pounded as she listened to the melancholy sounds. How could a carol of joy be played with such infinite sadness?

Suddenly, tears flooded her eyes and she felt them running cold down her face. She clenched her fists in her pockets, hunched her shoulders, and let the music wash over her, tear into her, cut her heart to ribbons.

"Don't!" she said harshly, and the music came to a discordant stop. "Oh, Lord, please stop it!" She realized that she was standing before Marc Duval and had no idea how she had gotten there. He had come to his feet, had shoved his harmonica into the pocket of his leather jacket, and was staring at her. "Don't!" she cried again, her voice breaking. "I can't bear it another minute! Just stop torturing me, Duval! Stop!"

Two

"What is it?" Marc demanded. "What's wrong, Sharon?" He'd never called her by her first name, except in the conversations he made up in his head. It felt so good, he said it again with all the tenderness she evoked in him. "Sharon . . ." He reached out to touch one of the silver streaks tracking down her face. "Don't cry, little Sharon." Lord, but she was lovely by moonlight, even weeping, even angry she stirred his soul.

She gasped and flinched at his touch as if he had slapped her. Jumping back, she tripped on the edge of the concrete pad the camper sat on. She would have fallen, but he caught her around the waist and drew her hard against him.

Sharon trembled at the contact, holding herself stiffly, waiting for him to let her go. He did not, but instead lifted his hand again and wiped the tears from her cheek, making her heart pound at the feel of him against her, at the shocking eroticism of his rough, callused palm on her cheek. Unable to stop herself, she leaned into it just a little, turned her head a fraction of an inch, seeking the contact.

"Don't!" she said brokenly, her gaze pleading.

"Don't what? Don't touch your skin, even though your eyes beg me to do it? Don't play Christmas music because it makes you sad and lonely? I was feeling that way, too, Sharon." He paused, as if considering just what he should say. "We're both so alone! But if we were . . . friends, then neither of us would have to feel that way again."

"Friends?" She tipped her head back and stared at him intently. "We can't be friends!"

He lifted his brows so they disappeared under the front of his moon-gilded hair. "Why not?"

Her voice trembled. "Because you won't leave me alone! You come to the library all the time and talk to me, make me—" Make her what, she didn't say, but he could guess. He knew what she made him feel and was certain it was the same for her. "You won't stop playing your instruments outside my house," she went on, "and you are driving me to distraction! Music, music, music, all day long and half the night! It isn't fair! I just wish you had never come here! I wish you would go away! You have no right to disturb my life like this! You are—" She broke off abruptly, her eyes filling with terror as she struggled in his gentle hold, her breath rasping in and out.

"I'm sorry, I'm sorry," she said, sounding panic-stricken. "I . . . Just let me go, Mr. Duval. I'll go home. I shouldn't have come. I'll just go inside, and I won't have to hear you play and—"

"Now I know," he said softly, interrupting her staccato speech. "Now I know why you dislike me so much."

His words quelled her panic, but she still needed her freedom from him, space in which to breathe. She placed her hands against the thick woolen sweater that covered his chest, thinking sourly that he might clean up nicely, but he sure didn't stay that way any longer than he had to. She pushed, but it was like shoving against a cliff. "I . . . I never said I disliked you, Mr. Duval. Let me go now, please. I won't bother you again."

He didn't let her go, but slipped his other arm behind her, and leaned back against the metal wall of the camper. "You bother me all the time, Sharon Leslie, and you didn't have to tell me that you don't like me. It's there every time we meet, blazing from your eyes. It's the music, isn't it? It reminds you too much of what you gave up."

"No! Of course not! I never gave up anything! Or, if I did, I did it because I wanted to. Music nearly ruined my life, my children's lives. I don't want it anymore!"

"Do you hate all musicians because you're a failed one yourself?" He ignored her gasp of indignation and went on. "If that's the case, you have no need to hate me. I'm not a real musician. I'm only an amateur." If making her angry or indignant, even hurting her a little was the way through that wall, then he would take it. Inside, part of him rejoiced that she had come to him, even if only to beg him to stop torturing her with music.

He didn't yet understand how music could be a torture to her of all people, although he could see that it was. Since he'd come, he supposed, every time he had sat outside and played quietly to keep himself company, her suffering had grown stronger. Those tears had been genuine, her anguish deep and real. But why? And why had she stopped composing? Why had she stopped playing? The glory she had wrung from that harp earlier had enchanted him totally, filled him with wonder. She was so talented! He knew that in spite of what he had said, she was no failed musician, but what he needed to know was why she had given it up.

He didn't think she was likely to tell him then, so he gently eased his arms away from her, setting her free. "I'll stop playing where you can hear me if it bothers you so much, Sharon."

"I . . . thank you. I apologize for my rudeness. I should have just gone inside and shut the door so I couldn't hear. It was wrong of me to come over here."

"You're welcome here anytime. As are your children."

"My children." Her eyes flew to his face, suddenly fiercely defiant and startlingly bright. "Just remember, Mr. Duval, that they are *my* children. I don't want you to offer Jason guitar lessons. I don't want you to encourage him to take an interest in music. I want him and Roxanne to grow up knowing that there are other things in life as important as music . . . more important. Much more!"

"Nothing was more important to you for most of your life, Sharon. Why do you deny your son his enjoyment of it? If you don't want him to come to like my kind of music, why don't you give him yours, which is far superior?"

"Why don't you mind your own damned business!" she said, and then bit her lip and dropped her head, stepping back slightly. "I'm sorry, Mr. Duval. That was rude." She looked at him again, all defiance gone. "Listen, all I'm asking is that you leave my son alone. Please try to understand that he's at a very vulnerable stage of his development. He needs a man to look up to, and you're not the kind of man I want him to emulate."

He frowned. Did she know about him? He shook his head. How could she? No! There was simply no way! "Why not?" he asked, picking up the conversation.

"Well . . . because you're a . . . drifter. A wanderer. You've told Jason about all the places you've stayed, a few days here, a few weeks there, and now you're here. For a while."

"I've been here longer than anyplace else," he pointed out.

"And when spring comes, you'll be on your way again. I don't want him to come to . . . rely on you."

"Would you deny your son friendship because he might not keep it forever? Is that why you deny yourself love?"

"What?" Her black eyes shone with deep lights as they opened wide and caught the moonlight. "What gives you the right to make such an assumption about me?"

"Your actions, Ms. Leslie. Your attitudes."

"Who are you to speak of 'attitudes'? And we were discussing my son, not me, his friendships and needs, not mine."

"So what kind of a man do you want to set an example for your son? That tight-faced banker I've seen you with?"

"Why not? He's a good man. Kind, steady, leads a settled life. He's—" *Safe*, she had been going to say, but he broke into her brief hesitation before she could come up with the word.

"He's what? Dull? Boring?"

She looked away from him. There was nothing she could say, really. Lorne Cantrell was dull and boring, but he was also what she was looking for:

someone who would never be able to hurt her. She knew that she wasn't risking hurt with him because she could make no real emotional commitment. However, she didn't care about that. She might, in time, be able to make a practical commitment to him. She could be a part-time mother to his children. She would learn to care for them. He could be a full-time father to hers. They would come to like him, and to get along with his children. What she had to look for was security, calm—a serene, quiet atmosphere in which to raise her kids. No ups, no downs, just nice, level, even-paced family living.

"Do you want dull, Sharon? Do you want boring? Or do you want this," Marc said, his voice a low growl as he pulled her into his arms again. "I can see it in your eyes, Sharon, how you want me. I can feel it in the tension of your body whenever I come and stand by your desk in the library, or stand in line behind you at the post office. I can hear it in your breathing right now. You want me. I know that because I want you, too, and someday, you are going to admit it freely."

"No!" she said, but when his mouth came slowly toward hers, she did not turn her head away. She stared at him, mesmerized, until his lips brushed over hers, back and forth, until need and curiosity overcame caution and her own parted so she could taste and feel him with the tip of her tongue. Then her eyes fell closed as her body grew heavy and warm, curling toward his like a flower to the sun.

Her breasts pressed against the hardness of his chest and swelled with an aching need for even greater closeness. A deep, silent part of her cried out with exhilaration at the worship she sensed in his touch, in celebration of the way she felt as he unzipped her jacket and slid his arms inside it, molding her shape with his big hands. It had been so long since she had felt like a real woman, a woman who might be able to satisfy a man. And something told her that this time, she could. She yearned to have his hands on her bare skin, all over her, touching, stroking, arousing. Oh, heavens, but he felt good against her, hard and big and masculine! She shoved her cold hands inside his leather jacket, into his warmth. He smelled wonderful, the way a man should, and tasted incredible, of oranges and mint. She let her head fall back against his hand as it came from inside her jacket and rose to slide through her hair.

At once something turbulent, too long pent up, was unleashed in both of them, and they both met it without hesitation.

She moved against him, reveling in the solidness of his frame. *Oh, Lord,* she thought dimly, *I've needed this man for so long!* And then she no longer thought but simply gave herself up to the pleasures she and Marc Duval were drawing from each other, creating in each other, building together.

Her hair was like black silk as it slid through his fingers. Marc took all the sweetness her mouth offered, accepting the tentative little forays her tongue made against his own, then groaning as she became emboldened and moved deeper into his embrace, her mouth hungry and demanding under his. She clung to him, her hands clenching in his hair as if to pull him deep inside her skin. He strained to get closer, closer, but it could never be close enough, not like this, fully clothed, standing outside under a Christmas moon.

He had known! From the moment he'd first met

her sultry gaze, seen it fire up and crackle at him, he had known there would be this kind of spark between them, a spark that would turn into instant conflagration. He wanted her like he had never wanted another woman in all of his forty-one years. He wanted to strip her down to her bare skin, lay her on the cold hard ground, and drive himself into her again and again until the desperate urge to have her was finally sated. But he knew that kind of urge would never be fully quenched. He lifted her up off her feet to rub her against him. When she moved her slight, dainty body, parted her legs to make a cradle for his arousal, he groaned and nearly collapsed as his knees gave way. He set her swiftly back onto her feet and turned aside to save his sanity, reluctantly breaking their heated kiss.

When he lifted his head, he couldn't speak, could only look at her. She was so beautiful with the moon shining on her pale face, her black lashes contrasting arcs along her skin, her lips wet and parted as if begging for more. But not now. He couldn't give her more. He knew if he took those lips again, he would gather her up and take her to his bed in the camper. At this point, maybe she wouldn't object, but when it was over, so would be his every chance of earning her trust. Wanting was one thing, friendship another, and he knew he would have to have both from her before he could even think of telling her his story.

"Angel," he murmured finally, "open your eyes. Look at me."

She did, and he saw that she was still dazed by the desire that had flared so swiftly and so powerfully between them. The stars high above reflected in the deep pools of her dark eyes. "I want you to go in now, Sharon," he lied. He didn't want her to go in. He wanted to keep her with him, enfolded in his arms, and make her so hot the cold wouldn't matter. "It's cold out here. It's time you were in your bed."

She looked at him for a long moment, blinking as she remembered who she was, where she was, and who he was. "Mr. Duval . . ." Sharon unclenched her hands from the wool of his sweater, pulled them from under the front of his jacket, and moved back from him, out of his circle of warmth. Her breathing was shallow and rapid. Her head spun. Her brain felt like mashed potatoes. She didn't know what to say to him. If he hadn't brought their untamed kisses to a halt, she willingly would have made love with him right there. Even now, she ached with a terrible need that she knew he could fill. "Mr. Duval . . ." she tried again, but once more there were no words she could say.

"Don't you think you could start to call me Marc now?" he asked softly, taking her hands and tenderly tucking them into the pockets of her blue jacket, then zipping the front of it up to her chin. He smiled. "You can't exactly call us strangers after that . . ."

"I . . . guess not." She swallowed hard and drew in a deep, shaky breath. She had to regain control of her own senses. She remembered all too well what happened to a woman who allowed herself to become so sexually overwhelmed that she couldn't make herself turn and walk away from a man. Marc Duval was one man who could do that to her. And she was not going to permit it.

"Good night," she said, and as she spoke, the bell in the church steeple a few miles away began to chime the midnight hour. They stood together, not touching, listening in silence to the bell, gazing down the valley toward the church. When the last, deep-throated, resounding "bong" had faded away into the night, she whispered, almost as if in surprise, "It's Christmas Day."

"I'll walk you home," he said.

She smiled, and his heart swelled at this first real grin Sharon Leslie had ever given him. "It's only a few feet."

"Still, I'll make sure you're safely inside." He took her arm and walked with her, careful not to brush his shoe against the white fur at the hem of her gown. At her door, he turned her and looked down into her face.

"Merry Christmas, Sharon."

She gave him another smile, just a tiny one, but enough to fill him with happiness he'd forgotten he could feel. "Good night . . . Marc. Merry Christmas."

"Mommy! Look! Wake up! Look what Santa Claus put in my stocking!"

Sharon groaned as she rolled over and blinked her eyes open, trying to focus on what Roxy had shoved right under her nose. Grasping her daughter's hand, she put it back at least a foot so she could see the object, and smiled at Roxanne's delight.

"My Little Pony!" Roxy exulted, as if her mother wouldn't recognize the toy. "Santa must have known I lost my other one somewhere. Look, Mommy, here's a bunch of barrettes and a whole big box of Smarties! Do I have to share those, or are they all for me?"

"They're all for you, sweetheart. Merry Christmas. Climb in here and keep warm while you see what else Santa put in your stocking. Is Jason up yet?" She hoped he wasn't; maybe, after she'd seen the contents of her fat, bulging stocking, Roxy would be content to go to sleep again. A glance at her bedside clock told Sharon that it wasn't yet five o'clock. It had been well after midnight when she'd finally gone to bed, and then she hadn't been able to sleep for hours, thinking of those incredible moments in Marc Duval's arms. What a fool she'd been to let something like that happen! What a stupid risk she'd taken!

Cuddled with her little daughter, she drifted off again and didn't awaken until Jason came in at half past seven, eyes shining with pleasure at the contents of his stocking, even though he knew full well who had stuffed it the night before. The three of them sat in Sharon's big bed and gloated over the goodies until they heard the McKenzie family up and moving around.

They opened their gifts before breakfast, the adults fortified with plenty of hot coffee, the children needing no fortification at all.

As she rolled her toy bulldozer across the carpet back toward the tree, her new doll riding astride it, Roxy looked over her shoulder at her mother, sitting in a nest of crumpled paper and shining bows and tangled ribbons. "Do you think Auntie Jeanie's feeling lonely for us this morning?"

She knew Roxy missed her aunt. This was her first Christmas without Jeanie. "I'm sure she is, honey. But we'll all be together again next Christmas." Behind her, Sharon heard a chuckle and looked at Rolph, whose green eyes danced with merriment as they shared a smile. He had a bright red scarf wrapped around his neck, even though he was wearing a pair of pajamas covered by a bathrobe. Freda had given it to him, and he wanted to wear it right away.

"I doubt Jeanie's even aware it's Christmas," he murmured.

Beside him, Harry laughed softly and said, "Max, on the other hand, probably thinks it's Christmas and Easter and every birthday he's ever had, all rolled into one. Your turn next, number two son."

"Amen to that," said Freda, stroking the soft plush of a new bathrobe one of the boys had given her.

Rolph shrugged. "So find me someone who's interested for more than fifteen minutes, and I might just take your suggestion seriously. After all, even though I caught the garter you didn't see any eligible females flinging themselves at my feet, did you?"

Sharon remembered how Marian Crane, the sharp-tongued, witty redhead who'd ducked the bouquet, had looked at Rolph when he caught that shocking-pink garter. She wondered if Rolph even knew that she was interested in him and probably had been for a long time. She also wondered if it was Rolph's habit of treating her like a sister that had made Marian deliberately duck the flowers.

Zinnie shook her head at him in disgust. "Right. You caught the garter, for all the good it'll do you. You've always given up too easily, my son. The day you try longer than fifteen minutes, *I'll* begin to take *you* seriously. No, Sharon's the next one. She caught the bouquet. By the way, did anybody else hear that nice Mr. Duval playing carols on his harmonica last night? It was a lovely sound to fall asleep to."

Sharon jumped up from the floor and began collecting her gifts and moving the piles back under the tree. "Breakfast time," she said. "If we don't get that out of the way so I can get the turkey stuffed and into the oven, we'll be eating Christmas dinner sometime tomorrow morning."

Jason grinned. "Mom, you say that every year."

"That's because every year we linger under the tree far too long." Then, robe flying out around her, she spun from the group in the living room and went swiftly into the kitchen. She'd get dressed after breakfast.

Looking out the window, she saw a silver world with the dazzle of frost on grass and shrubs, the sun peeking over the treetops to add a hint of sparkle. It was a beautiful Christmas morning, the closest thing to a white Christmas she'd ever seen there on the coast. Snow, if it came down to sea level, usually did so in January. Leaning forward just a bit, she could see the camper with its windows steamed up, and stood clutching the edge of the sink, thinking about Marc Duval again.

It was his breath that had caused that steam. What would the windows look like if there had been two of them in there last night as there so nearly had been, if he hadn't been the one to call a halt? She shivered and rubbed her arms under the wide sleeves of her robe, encountering her half dozen of Grandma Margaret's gold bangles she still wore. She'd forgotten to take them off the previous night. Now, slipping them down over her hand, she reached to set them on the windowsill just as the door of Marc's camper opened. He stepped out, looked right at her, and smiled. At that moment, one of the bangles fell into the sink with a musical tinkle, and inside Sharon something turned over and came to life again. She spun away from the window, forcing the feeling down with all her might.

"No way, Grandma Margaret! I don't care what you did to Jeanie. You're not doing the same thing to me. Not until I find a man I know is absolutely right. And Marc Duval is absolutely, completely, and terribly wrong."

"What's that, dear?" Freda asked behind her, coming in fully dressed and ready for the day. "Did you say something was wrong?" Shoving up her sleeves, Freda added, "Never mind. What could be wrong on such a perfect Christmas morning? You start the bacon, dear. I'll take care of toast and eggs."

The table was set on white lace over red linen. Silverware gleamed. China shone. Crystal twinkled merrily with the reflected lights of the tree in the living room beyond. The wonderful aroma of roasting turkey filled the house. Sharon added the finishing touches to the table and joined her new family in the living room.

The children sat on the floor, laughing, talking, playing with their new toys. Harry and Freda were doing a jigsaw puzzle, while Zinnie and Rolph rested on a big sofa, enjoying each other's company. In the background, a record of the Mormon Tabernacle Choir played, permeating the room with the spirit of Christmas.

Did hearing me play make you feel lonely and sad? Marc Duval's voice resounded in her ears as if he had stepped into the room and spoken those words from the previous night. Sharon sighed and sat down in a chair between Harry and Freda, picked up a puzzle piece, tried it, found it didn't fit, and leaned back, lost in thought. What was he doing right now? Was he sitting in his camper, feeling lonely and blue? What must it be like to spend Christmas Day all alone? He had said he might be moving into the house today. What a way to spend Christmas, and how long would that take, anyway? The Hardings had always rented the house fully furnished; she supposed he had bought it that way. What would he have to move but a few personal belongings? A banjo. A guitar. A flute. And a harmonica.

Christmas Day. Moving day. She frowned. She had never been completely alone at this time of year, but she had known the deepest kind of loneliness nevertheless. She swallowed the lump that rose into her throat.

How Jeanie would laugh if she knew she was sitting there mooning about the man next door! After all the trouble she'd gone to, dreaming up a man for her sister, going to the crazy extent of advertising for one, Jeanie had ended up falling in love with that dream man herself. She'd find it vastly amusing that Sharon had been doing far too much dreaming of her own since Marc Duval had come on the scene.

But, until the night before, she'd refused to let him get close; while she might want a man in her life, she did not want one who would demand too much of her either emotionally or sexually, and for that reason Marc Duval's very open attraction to her had to be quelled. Just as her most inappropriate responses to him had to be.

Besides, a handsome, sexy, interesting, and disturbing man did not necessarily make good husband material, and she still wanted to marry again. So, for her own sake, she would have to quit thinking about him, forget what they'd shared, forget that he was alone on Christmas Day.

Marc Duval was not her problem. Maybe he'd

gone out for the day. She knew he'd made friends since coming to town. Surely someone had invited him for dinner. As if to drive her crazy, the Mormon Choir began to sing "Silent night." Again she felt the deep melancholy that had no place in a home at Christmas. No, she told herself finally, it was better if she kept miles away from the man.

But what if nobody *had* asked him to dinner?

"What's the matter, Mom?"

She looked up, startled. Her son was standing right beside her. "Nothing, Jason. Why?"

"You sighed. You looked so sad for a minute." He frowned and continued, his voice low so no one else would hear, "You weren't thinking about *him*, were you?"

She put an arm around the boy and rested her head on his shoulder for a moment. "No, love. I wasn't thinking about your father." She smiled. "But you were, weren't you?"

He looked uncomfortable. "Maybe a little. Just sort of . . . remembering."

"Let's try not to, okay?"

She knew he was remembering that last, dreadful Christmas they had seen Ellis. She had hoped that time would blur the memories, but it had not. Perhaps they were too firmly ingrained in his mind ever to leave him completely. She was just grateful that Roxy, only three at the time, had no recollection of that terrible night, and that Jason, who'd been seven, remembered only that one. To her mind, the times they had been alone, without Ellis, had been as bad as the one Jason remembered. The loneliness she had suffered, the feelings of inadequacy, the yearning for something that she had once thought would last forever had overwhelmed her. No human being should have to endure loneliness at this time of year, she realized.

Getting to her feet, she took Jason's hand and said, "Hey, let's you and I get our jackets and shoes on. There's something I want us to do together."

"What, Mom?"

"Never mind. Just come on. You'll see."

Moments later, Marc opened his door to a tentative knock. Jason stood there, beaming up at him. "Hi, Marc. Mom and I have come to invite you for dinner."

Over the boy's head, Marc sought out Sharon's fathomless dark eyes. Without a hint of a smile, she nodded, a curt little motion that caused her hair to swing down across her cheeks, partly obscuring the quick flare of color there.

"Thank you," he said, and the smile that lit his golden brown eyes was suddenly as precious to Sharon as any of the gifts she had received under the tree. "I can't think of anything I'd like better."

Three

When the doorbell rang, Sharon froze, feeling goosebumps rise up on her arms under the long sleeves of her dress. With her heart hammering high in her throat, she went into the foyer and opened the door, standing back so Marc could enter.

"You look beautiful," he said, eyes skimming over her black silk dress with its glittery red and silver bow pinned high on her left shoulder, and the red band holding her sleek hair back from her forehead. He handed her a brightly wrapped package, holding two more in the crook of his arm.

"Thank you," she said, for both the compliment and the gift. "But you certainly didn't have to do this. I didn't expect it."

"I know you didn't, any more than I expected your invitation. But I wanted to give you something. These are for the children."

"How nice of you. I'll call them."

"No. Not yet. I want to talk to you alone for just a moment." He lifted his free hand and touched her hair, then her cheek. His dark gold eyes were very serious. "Last night . . ." He swallowed. "Last night, what happened was important to me, Sharon. I want you to know that. I've wanted to hold you, touch you, kiss you, for a very long time. Ever since I first saw you. And I want to do it again," he added, almost in a whisper.

His soft voice got right inside her, twanging on nerve endings that should be left in peace, leaving her with a hot throbbing in the base of her abdomen. Fear struck her, fear that if he pushed this issue, she wouldn't be able to resist the crazy attraction between them any more than she had the previous night. She'd *liked* believing that it was only out of loneliness the incident had occurred. She'd finally gone to sleep convinced that mutual melancholy had driven them into each other's arms. Those kisses . . . Oh, Lord! She didn't want to remember them, but her body wouldn't forget. Still, she had to fight it.

"Marc . . . please. It shouldn't have happened. It won't, not again." And it wouldn't, she promised herself. Because if it did, if she allowed herself to listen to the dictates of her body rather than her mind, she'd get all tangled up in an affair with him, and then she'd never find the kind of man she really needed and wanted, someone she could care for in an easy, detached manner, someone who would be good not only for her, but for her children. If not Lorne Cantrell, then someone very much like him.

"It will, you know," he said, and bent to brush her lips softly with his. "We won't be able to stop it now. Either of us." She jerked back, covering her mouth with one hand, her eyes wide and stormy.

"Don't!" she said. "I thought I had made myself clear. I do not want that from you."

"Don't lie to me, Sharon," he said with a slow, sexy smile that turned her inside out. "And above all, don't lie to yourself."

She turned and left the entry where they had been secluded. She could feel him close behind her, then the kids saw him and he crouched to hug Roxy and place an affectionate hand over Jason's head.

"Open them, go ahead," he urged, once he'd given the children their gifts.

Jason looked sorrowful. "But we don't have anything for you, Marc."

Over Jason's head, Marc's gaze met Sharon's. "I've already had all I want for Christmas this year." He smiled at the boy who was looking down into a box of huge homemade chocolate chip cookies.

"Wow!" Jason's eyes were wide. "Did you make these?"

"I did. I hope you like them."

"Love them!" Turning to his mother, he said, "Can I have one now?"

She nodded.

Roxy found cookies in her package as well, big thick ones filled with raspberry jam. Her eyes closed in bliss as she bit into one and chewed, a look of delight on her piquant face. "How come a daddy can make cookies?" she asked.

"I like baking cookies," Marc said. Then he asked Sharon, "Aren't you going to open yours?"

"Oh!" She had forgotten she held it in her hand. "Of course. But come in, sit down. You remember Harry McKenzie, I'm sure."

"What a pleasure to see you again, Mr. Duval. Sharon mentioned that you'd be joining us. I've been delegated as bartender this evening. What can I get for you while we wait for dinner?"

"A cola would be fine, Mr. McKenzie. Thanks."

"Harry."

"Right. And I'm Marc." He sat beside Sharon on the sofa and watched as eagerly as her children while she undid the wrapping with care and revealed a beautiful, polished shell about three inches long. It was a delicate shade of pinkish gray, with deeper violet spots on the ribs of its whorls.

"Oh . . ." It was a small sound of pure pleasure, and it warmed Marc right through, as did the shine of the gaze she lifted to him. "Thank you. It's the most beautiful shell I've ever seen. Where did you find it?" She couldn't have said how she knew he hadn't bought it in a store, but something about his manner told her that he had picked up this one himself in his travels and had kept it because he liked it. And now he had given it to her.

"I was diving off a little island near Oahu," he said. "They live quite deep as a rule, so I was lucky to find this one in about sixty feet of water."

She picked it up and cradled it in her hand, brushing one finger over the satin-smooth texture of its inner surface. "Thank you, Marc. You couldn't have thought of anything I'd have liked better. Do you know what it's called?"

He smiled, so delighted she liked his gift that he wanted to crush her in his arms and kiss her until they were both out of breath—but not with an audience present. "I think it's a harp shell." He accepted a glass of iced cola from Harry without taking his eyes from Sharon's glowing face. How long they might have sat there just looking at each other, saying potent and silent things,

Sharon had no idea, but fortunately they were interrupted.

"Hello, Marc. How nice to see you." Zinnie came from the kitchen, and he stood quickly, only sitting again when she'd perched on the arm of the sofa. "What's that you have there, Sharon? My, my! What a rare specimen. Did you collect it yourself, Marc?"

"Merry Christmas, Mrs. McKenzie, and yes, I did. Are you a serious shell collector?"

She smiled and said, "I guess you could call me a serious shell collector. I'm a marine biologist and specialize in mollusks."

"Oh." He gave his little one-sided shrug and looked apologetic. "Then I guess I should call you Dr. McKenzie?"

"I guess you should call me Zinnie, unless you're looking for a fat lip," she said with a grin. "I came out to tell you that Freda says the gravy is at its peak of perfection, Sharon. There's nothing modest about Freda, let me say. Do you want Harry to carve at the table or in the kitchen? Would one of you kids go and see if your uncle Rolph is coming out or if he wants his dinner served in there beside your video games."

Both children took off down the hall toward the TV room, where Rolph had spent much of the afternoon with them playing with the new games, as happy as any ten-year-old.

Sharon laid her pretty shell carefully back into its nest of tissue and set the box with her other gifts. "I'd better get back on duty," she said with a smile for everyone. She didn't dare meet Marc's gaze again.

"If you don't mind having your talents on display, Harry, I'd love to have you carve at the table. It seems to do so much for the appetite."

"You got it, baby doll," he said. "Shall I uncork the wine now?"

"Yes, please. Excuse me, won't you? Dinner will be just a few minutes."

As she stood and walked past Marc, she caught a faint whiff of his after-shave and was sure her knees would buckle before she could get safely away. What a mistake it had been to invite the man for dinner! Clearly he had misinterpreted her neighborly gesture as an invitation to repeat their foolishness. But she wouldn't. Somehow, she would keep up her firm resolve. All she had to do was quit looking at him.

"How did a marine biologist and a civil engineer manage two such disparate careers?" Marc asked, accepting his well-stocked plate back from Harry.

"While I was off in the bush building bridges, Zinnie was lounging on beaches, waiting for the waves to wash in a shell or two," Harry said, earning an indignant look from his wife.

"What he means to say is that while I was diving into treacherous waters, risking my life and the bends to collect specimens of bivalve mollusks for the advancement of higher learning, he was lolling in hammocks strung between trees, bossing a crew of the *real* bridge builders."

Everyone had turkey on their plates now, and the vegetable dishes had made their rounds. After a brief prayer, Sharon lifted her glass and said, "To Christmas, friends, and family."

Everyone responded, lifting their glasses, and then Harry said, "To our hostess."

"Our hostess," came the response, and from somewhere to her left, Sharon distinctly heard the word "beautiful" added to the toast. Against her will, she glanced at Marc, meeting his gaze as he lifted his glass to his lips. To her surprise, he did not drink, but set the glass down again. With a smile, he picked up his fork as she had done.

"It must have been difficult to be away from your family," she said quickly to Zinnie, taking the conversation back in the direction it had been going before the toasts.

"It was, but luckily we've always had Freda."

"Yes," said Freda. "While they were off on their little junkets to warm, exotic, and interesting places, I was at home tending their wicked sons, trying to turn them into decent human beings." She reached across the table and patted Rolph's hand. "And look what we ended up with!"

"But just think, Freda, if you hadn't stayed home and looked after us, we might have grown up in some of those exotic and interesting places and become even more wicked. Think what your sacrifices have meant to the world."

"I remind myself of it every day," said the elderly lady, "and I know heaven will reward me. But speaking of warm and exotic places, Marc, I saw that shell you gave to Sharon. She tells me you've traveled much of the world. What do you do?"

Sharon's ears pricked up at that. She had wondered more than once exactly what it was Marc did. Her imagination had suggested everything from drug importer to spy.

"A little of this, a little of that," he said with an easy smile. "I learned how to bake cookies when I worked in a bakery in New Zealand." He spoke directly to the children, then added, "I took up diving in Fiji and worked there leading snorkling tours for a while before shipping out on a freighter to Japan, where I spent several months."

"Wow!" Jason said, leaning forward eagerly. "Did you jump ship?"

"No." Marc laughed. "I had only signed on that far. I wanted to see some of the Orient. I just bummed around for a few months in Japan, in Hong Kong, and in mainland China, then caught a ride on a sailboat that was coming back this way shorthanded. I wasn't much value to the skipper for the first week, with my head hanging over the rail, but I enjoyed the rest of the trip and learned a lot about sailing. So much that I crewed again, all the way back across the Pacific."

"Where else have you been? What else have you done? It sounds as if you've led a fascinating life," said Zinnie.

"I've done so many things, I can't remember them all. I tend to work at something until it's not fun anymore, then go on to something else. Living that way, I've seen a good portion of the world. But here's something I've been wondering about, and now that I'm at the same table as a marine biologist, maybe I can get an answer. I was wondering if you'd know about gray whales . . ."

Zinnie did know, and the conversation ranged then from the habits of the different species of whales to how stress factors have to be worked into bridges in high-risk earthquake regions, and what color upholstery fabric is most pleasing to the owners of ocean-going yachts, but it never managed to stay long on what Marc Duval had done with his life.

He was being deliberately evasive, Sharon concluded, the third or fourth time he deflected the conversation, and when he disappeared into the kitchen with Rolph and Harry, who claimed it was a tradition in the McKenzie household that the men clean up after the women had done the cooking, she told herself she was glad to see him go.

Freda and Zinnie were working on the jigsaw again, wanting to see it completed before they had to leave in the morning, and Sharon had just come down from getting the children into bed when the men returned. She was sitting staring idly into the fire, listening to the murmured conversation going on behind her at the card table. Marc sat beside her, as if it were his rightful place to be.

"Will you play for us?" he asked softly, and she flinched away from him.

"No!" It was a sharply whispered refusal.

"Why not?" He spoke in a normal conversational tone, drawing everyone's attention their way. "I'd like to hear you play again."

"Oh, Sharon, please. Hearing you yesterday was such a treat," said Freda.

Yesterday? For a moment, she couldn't remember what Zinnie meant. For some reason that whole day seemed far in the past. "No. I'm sorry. I don't want to. I don't play anymore."

"You played at your sister's wedding."

"That was different. It was a promise I'd made. I had to."

Marc looked at her intently, speaking as if the two of them were alone. "I know I'm only a guest in your home, Sharon, but we've enjoyed a traditional Leslie family dinner, done a traditional McKenzie family cleanup in the kitchen, and now I'd like to add a Duval tradition to this very wonderful Christmas you were so kind to share with me." He smiled at her, and her stomach flipped over a few times before it settled down. Her heart, however, speeded up alarmingly.

"What tradition is that?"

"After dinner—which, by the way, we always had on Christmas Eve—we sang carols while my mother played the piano. That was what I was missing last night when I played my harmonica."

Her throat tightened. "I see."

"If I brought it over, could you all sing carols?"

"I . . . yes. Of course." She looked at her harp in its corner. "But . . ."

He touched her cheek with one bent finger. "No one will insist. If you want to, do it. If you don't . . . then . . ." The shrug he gave was entirely Gallic, as was the one-sided smile.

"It would be nice to sing carols together. I just wish the kids hadn't both been so tired."

"There'll be other times for them. This time is for us." He still held her gaze as he got to his feet. She knew that when he said "us" he was not including the McKenzies.

He was back moments later with both guitar and harmonica, and began playing the latter softly, as if to set a mood. "Sing," he urged them, and they did, tentatively at first, then with confidence as their voices blended nicely.

While he took a break and drank another glass of pop, Zinnie asked, "Do you come from a large family, Marc?"

He smiled. "Oh, yes. There are seven of us. I spoke to my parents and a couple of my brothers and sisters last night, but it was too hard to hear much with all the kids shouting in the background."

Sharon stared at her hands in her lap. Why, she wondered, did a man with such a large and presumably close family, choose to spend Christmas alone in a camper?

Zinnie, bless her, was wondering, too, and not at all averse to asking, however tactfully. "So sad, you can't be with them this year."

"Yes," was all he said as he picked up the guitar in place of the harmonica, and began strumming the strains of "White Christmas."

"You sing too," Zinnie said, but he shook his head.

"I learned to play instruments because I sound like a sick old crow when I sing. But I'm enjoying your voices."

Presently, Rolph slipped away, giving Sharon a quick smile and a wave as he headed for the stairs, then Freda, too, retired. For another half hour, Harry and Zinnie sat and listened quietly to the guitar, then rose and excused themselves.

Sharon thought Marc would go, too, but he continued to play.

"I like sitting here with you, watching the fire die," he said, still strumming a delicate chord. "I could spend a lot of evenings like this without getting tired of it."

"But one day you would, and then you'd be gone."

"Would that matter to you so very much?"

She was silent, listening to the music, feeling it in her blood, filled with an almost uncontrollable need to go to her harp and play. She had once found such solace in music, and then it had become a punishment, a chore. She never wanted to feel with that kind of intensity again. "It . . . could. If I let it."

He stood the guitar on its end, leaning against the arm of the couch. "Will you?"

"Will I . . . ?"

"Let it matter. Let me matter."

She shook her head. "Marc, I can't. It would be too . . . dangerous."

"Why do you say that? How am I a danger to you? What makes you so afraid?"

"Who you are. What you are."

Again, he was startled, taken aback. *Did* she know who he was? There was no way it was possible, but he had to find out.

"All right then." His mouth was dry. "Who am I? What am I?"

"That's just it. I don't know. You came out of nowhere, and out of everywhere. You have no visible means of support, yet you dress like this"— she reached out and brushed the back of her fingers down the sleeve of his well-cut, clearly expensive suit—"when the occasion warrants it. You come and go at will, living in a battered camper on the back of a rusty pickup, yet you buy a house that I'm sure didn't sell for peanuts. And none of this is any of my business, but I like to know who I'm dealing with."

She swallowed. "At dinner, whenever anyone asked you what you did, you evaded the issue. I don't like evasions. To me, they are as bad as lies." For too long, she had suffered from a man's lies and evasions.

"Are you asking me what I do for a living?"

She sighed. "Yes. I suppose I am."

"I'm a cookie-maker."

She got to her feet. "Marc . . ."

He rose and turned her to face him. "No, seriously, that's what I am now. I've opened a cookie bakery in Victoria, another in Vancouver, and I'm working on a third in Seattle. I think that's probably what I'll do with the rest of my life. Make cookies."

"But you don't actually make them yourself!"

"The ones I brought to your kids, I did. From my mother's old recipes. That's what the ones in my bakeries are based on too. I sell direct to university and college cafeterias, to day-care centers and hospitals, and certain select, small stores. It's a good marketing ploy, keeping my product exclusive until there's a real following. Then, when the time is right, and I'm sure quality control can be maintained, I might branch out into wider markets."

"Then why live here? Why Nanaimo? Why not Vancouver or Victoria or Seattle?"

"I like it here. It's a big enough town to have a few amenities, yet small enough to be friendly. Big cities are—" He broke off, frowning. "Big cities are part of my past, and I prefer to leave that where it lies, behind me."

"I've noticed."

"I'm sorry. There are things I don't want to talk about. I'm not being evasive now, and I wasn't being evasive at dinner. I have done all those things I said, have been to all those places, and I did learn to bake cookies in New Zealand. I even taught my boss to make some of my mother's recipes. It was the way they went over there that suggested to me maybe I could earn a living with them if I ever came home."

"But you aren't 'home,' " she said, moving restlessly away from him, crouching to put another couple of pieces of wood on the fire. She shut the glass doors and stood again, facing him with a much safer distance between them.

"Why do you say that?"

"Your accent. Where is home? Somewhere in Quebec?"

"It was. It no longer is. Now, home is where I want it to be." He moved closer, not touching her. "I want it to be here, Sharon."

"For the time being. Until cookies aren't fun any longer." *Until I'm not interesting enough any longer.*

He frowned. "Maybe. I don't know. Over the last few months I've come to realize that this might well be where I will settle, that cookies might well be what I'll want to make my life's work." He paused, stroked a hand over her hair. "Those months, too, of knowing you—at least, seeing you, talking to you now and then—have told me that maybe I'd like you to be part of that life."

She laughed and shook his hand off her hair. "I don't bake cookies worth a damn!"

His smile warmed her right to the soles of her feet in a way she didn't want it to. "So Jason tells me. I told him you have other, more important talents."

Together, as if pulled by a magnet, their gazes swept to her harp. She shook her head. "No. No more."

He took one of her hands and pulled her a step closer to him. Their bodies touched lightly. Her heart raced. Her breath caught in her throat. "Will you tell me about it? What happened? What changed you? Was it your divorce? Did it hurt you so badly that you died inside and your music died with you?"

She shook her head. "Not that. I was . . . glad for the divorce. It eased my hurts. My music died long before that. At least, the music in my heart did. I kept on playing though, trying to find it again. Finally, I just gave up."

"Funny," he said musingly, "when my wife and son died, I thought everything good in me had died too, but music, which I've always treasured, lived on, and eventually gave me some comfort . . ."

Her eyes opened wide. "You lost your family? Oh, Marc, I am so sorry."

He flicked at one of the tears that spilled from the corner of her eye. "Don't cry for me. It's all in the past. I want to look to the future. And last night gave me hope that maybe I can have the future I want."

"Last night was . . ." Her voice trailed away.

"Was what?" he asked softly, lifting her face up, cupping his hands around it. "As magical for you as it was for me?"

His hands, hard and callused, which had felt erotic the previous night, felt different somehow, reminding her of the wide variety of tasks they had performed, and she knew he was still being evasive. He was no manual laborer, this man. Not with his understated elegance, his educated manner of speaking, his knowledge and savoir faire. He was a chameleon who was, in spite of his attraction to her, still avoiding telling her the truth about himself.

She would never let another dishonest man into her life!

"Don't *touch* me!" she said, jerking away from him.

The violence of her reaction, as well as the sudden flare of anger mixed with fear in her eyes, shook him as she tore herself free, wrapping her arms around herself. "Go home, Marc. Please, just go home now."

He picked up his guitar and his jacket and nodded. To the bowed back of her head, he said quietly, "All right, Sharon. We'll leave it for now. But I intend to know what happened to you. And I mean to make whatever went wrong, right."

She lifted her head, turned and looked at him, and the tragedy he read in her face made him want to weep for her as she had for him. "Nobody can, Marc. That's what you don't seem to understand. It can never be right again, so there's no point in my wanting a man like you—a man who would want too much."

He shook his head. "I'd never ask for more than you could give me."

"You would!" she protested, her mouth twisting. "You'd want everything."

"Yes," he agreed softly. "Of course I would. But why not? You *have* everything to give."

He slipped out the door then, leaving her standing at the archway to the entrance. After a moment, she locked the door behind her and went quietly up to bed.

She lay for a long time thinking about him, and soon it was morning and the whole house was stirring. She got out of bed quickly. There was no time for brooding. She had guests and children to feed, which was just as well. She'd never had much time for brooders. Action was what she preferred, and action was what she would take.

Four

"It's been a wonderful time, Sharon." Zinnie hugged her tightly as she and her family prepared to leave. "You gave your sister and our son a beautiful wedding and all of us a wonderful Christmas. It was more fun than we've had for a long time. You and your kids are a real bonus to us. What are you going to do with the rest of your holidays?"

"Today, we're going skiing, and we may go up again tomorrow, but the day after that, I'm afraid the library's open again, and I'll be working."

"Where do you ski?"

"Up Island. Mount Washington. It's the only one within reach for us, unless we want to stay over. Taking the ferry across to the mainland and back just eats up too much skiing time."

"You mean you'll drive up there today and back again tonight?" Harry asked, frowning. "Surely that eats up a lot of skiing time too."

"Well, yes, but it's what we have, so we make the best of it. Besides, the drive's no problem, since I don't have to travel in snow. I don't actually go up the mountain as a rule. They insist on chains, and I hate putting them on as much as I hate driving on snowy roads. There's a shuttle bus from the main parking lot. We use that."

"I know about the bus. We ski on Mount Washington, too, but listen, we have a chalet up there. Why don't you and the kids go on up and use it? That way you won't have to come back tonight, and you can have a full day's skiing tomorrow."

"Oh, but—"

"No, no buts. We insist," Zinnie said, digging into her capacious handbag and hauling out a ring of keys. Sorting through them, she found one and removed it, then slapped the key into Sharon's hand. "There. It's yours. Go ahead and enjoy." She explained how to find the chalet, and then added, "But listen, what plans do you have for the kids once you're back at work? What do they do?"

"I have a woman who comes in. She's really nice and they like her."

"Okay, but I have a better idea. What if we meet you up there tomorrow afternoon, and then stay on with the kids until the end of their Christmas vacation? We normally go up there for a few days at this time of year and spend New Year's Eve quietly on our own in the chalet. We'd really enjoy having the kids with us, though, wouldn't we, Harry?"

He beamed. "You bet! Hey, it's a long time since we've had kids up there. Come on, Sharon, say yes."

The two children stood there, big, dark eyes pleading with their mother, silently urging her to agree.

"But that's a terrible imposition!"

"Mom!" Two pained voices rang out.

"Imposition, nothing. We'll have a ball." Zinnie frowned. "Unless you don't feel you know us well enough yet to entrust us with your children. It's okay, dear. I understand."

"No! No, of course it's not that, Zinnie. After all we've been through together, those terrible days and nights of waiting for Jeanie and Max to be found? I feel I know you as well as I know my sister. Certainly I trust you with my kids, but it just seems like an awful lot to ask of you. They're very active and will wear you out."

"Hah!" said Freda with a sniff. "These two never wear out."

"It's true, Sharon." Rolph swung an arm around her, bumping her up against him in a brotherly fashion. "They ski circles around me every time we hit a mountain together. If I didn't have to fly to Lisbon tomorrow to look at that ketch of a client, I'd be joining them, and believe me, there's more than enough room for two little kids. Come on, whaddaya say, sis?"

"Ohhh!" Sharon felt tears flood her eyes and blinked hard to clear her vision. "You people are so darned good to us! Thank you. We accept."

"Great! Then we'll see you tomorrow afternoon. Don't bother packing any groceries except fresh stuff like milk and eggs. The cupboards and freezer are full, and we expect you to help yourself like any of the rest of the family. Understand?" Zinnie said.

And then the McKenzies were gone in a flurry of kisses and hugs and thanks. Sharon leaned back against the door and stared at her kids. "Wow!" she said. "What a super new family Aunt Jeanie brought us, huh?"

"Yeah," Jason said, his face aglow. "It's just like

having a grandma and grandpa must be, don't you think, Mom?"

She nodded and turned away quickly, busying herself so he wouldn't see the new spurt of tears in her eyes. There had been times over the past nineteen years when she had missed her own parents so desperately, she didn't know how she'd make it through another day. And now, it seemed, her sister's in-laws were going to make a very big stab at filling that huge gap in her life.

"Come on," she said. "Roxy, you collect up all the hats and gloves and goggles. Jase, you bring the skis up from the basement. I'll get the rack on top of the car. If we hurry, we can be on the slopes before lunch."

"Mommy, this is the best Christmas ever," Roxy said, leaning on her mother as they rode up in the chair lift. "I'm a good skier, now, aren't I?"

"You sure are. Better than last year. Here we go, time to dismount." Together they skied off the lift and headed down the hill after Jason, who had been in the chair ahead. Roxy was better than she'd been that morning, Sharon noticed. She was much more confident, more relaxed as they skied down Linton's Loop, a nice easy, relaxed run.

They had just reached the bottom and were taking a breather when a skier in a red and navy suit caught Sharon's eye. He came tearing down the face of the hill, over the steepest, most lumpy run, attacking the mountain as if it were an enemy, like a man possessed. Or a man in a great hurry. She frowned, wondering why so many men skied like that, and decided it was a male aggression thing, something they had to do. She had noticed signs of it in Jason.

The red and navy skier came directly toward them and swirled to a stop, lifting his goggles up over his headband, his tawny eyes laughing at her surprise. She did not feel nearly as surprised as she should, she realized, but instead felt a lot happier than was wise.

She knew he had seen her putting skis on the car earlier that morning. He had waved, and she had waved back. Then he'd gone inside, and she'd tried as usual to put him out of her mind.

"Hi, Marc!" Jason's gladness showed as he slid over to stand close to the man.

"Hi, yourself." Stabbing his poles into the snow to free his hands, Marc tugged Jason's hat down over his eyes. "Having a good time?"

Jason pushed his hat up onto his forehead again, his grin fading. "Okay, I suppose, but Mom won't let me ski the face like you just did. That was *excellent*! I didn't even know it was you, and I thought the guy was great. Have you been down the Westerly yet? I can't wait to go, but Roxy's too little for it."

"No. That was only my second run. I spotted you guys going up in the chair so I came down in a hurry to link up with you. Shall we take a run together?"

"Nah," Jason said disgustedly. "I gotta stick to the loop this year. 'Cause of my leg. The one I broke. The doctor said not to put too much strain on it or somethin'."

"That makes good sense, son. Anyway, I meant all of us together. The four of us. I don't suppose Roxy's ready yet for any of the more advanced runs." He grinned at the little girl who beamed back at him.

"But I will be next year. Mommy says I'm getting better all the time."

"And mommys are usually right, but let's see, shall we?" With that, he led the way to the line-up for the chair lift, maneuvering it somehow so that the kids took the chair ahead of him and Sharon.

"You look like a leprechaun in that green suit," he said.

She lifted an eyebrow. "I'm surprised a Frenchman knows about leprechauns."

"Ahh, but don't forget, I'm a widely traveled and very experienced Frenchman."

How experienced? Very, she was certain, didn't come close to covering it. She didn't want to think about that, though, about what he might know, things he might do, the way he so easily turned her inside out. "A Frenchman who learned to ski in Ireland, perhaps, where there are leprechauns?" she asked quickly.

"No, who learned to ski at Mont Ste.-Anne, in Quebec, where thy do not have leprechauns."

"So how would you know one if you saw one?"

"I've been to Ireland."

"Skiing?"

He laughed with her. "From what I saw, they don't even have any decent-sized mountains, though they do have some pretty craggy hills." He looked at her intently. "You're not Irish, are you?"

She laughed. "Heavens, no! My father's family came from Gypsy stock, and my mother's family are very staid and proper British people. In fact, my maternal grandfather was born in London, and my grandmother in Coventry. My mother was born on this side of the Atlantic, though, and while they tried very hard to make her into a proper little English girl, they had a hard row to hoe."

"Why is that?"

"I don't know if it was called peer pressure in those days, but she wanted to be just like the other kids on the block. She was a grave disappointment to them, just as Jeanie and I are."

"And your father?"

She smiled. Talking to him was easy, as long as they didn't get caught up in conversations that could lead to trouble. "His parents died young, too, so I just barely remember them."

"Do you remember your mother's parents?"

"Oh, yes. As a matter of fact, they live in Victoria, not far from the McKenzies."

"Oh. When you said that your father's parents died young, too, I thought you meant they had as well."

"I meant my parents. They died when I was eighteen."

"I see." His voice was gentle. "And your grandparents? Are they too old to travel?"

"No. I don't think so."

He frowned. "Yet they didn't attend your sister's wedding?"

"No," she said, watching her children dismount ahead of them, and readying herself to ski down the steep ramp. She stood, pushed off from the edge of the chair, and came to a stop at the end of the ramp where the kids were waiting. "All right," she said, "let's go." But as the children headed down the slope, her arm was caught in a fierce grip, pinning her where she stood.

"Why won't you talk about your family?"

Her gaze flew to his face. "I thought I just had."

"Your grandparents. They're alive, and yet when your son was lost, and then your sister, you were so alone except for Max's family. I used to sit in my camper after searching all day and think about you, about how alone you must be feeling. Yet you have family. Why weren't they with you?"

She looked up at him, then down at the large, gloved hand that held her arm. Slowly, he eased his grip and let her go with a murmured apology.

"You have family. Why weren't you with them for Christmas?"

"There are . . . reasons. Things I have yet to deal with."

"And there," she said, "is my answer to you. Only I don't intend to deal with them. My sister and I do not get along with our grandparents. They don't want to know about us and our lives, and we can live with that. End of story. Now, I came to ski. What did you come for?"

"The same as always. I came to be where you are." He held his position in front of her for another second, then leaned forward and brushed his mouth over her cold lips. They didn't remain cold long. The contact sent an electric shock and a bolt of heat through her.

With a firm shove on her poles, she shot back from him, turned quickly, and headed directly down the fall line, trying to catch up to her children.

With them, she would be safe. She watched Roxy navigate a steep bit of the slope like a pro, and thought how easily children relearned old lessons.

As a large form in a red jacket with blue sleeves caught up with her and skied beside her, she thought, too, how easily a woman's body could relearn things best forgotten. That short, hard kiss still burned her lips when she reached the foot of the slope, even though her cheeks stung with cold.

The four of them skied together for the rest of the afternoon, and Sharon couldn't remember when she'd enjoyed herself more. Not only was Marc an excellent skier who was more than willing to give both children impromptu lessons, but he had a sense of humor that could get her laughing and keep her that way until her sides ached. When she finally dragged her exhausted but reluctant children toward the chalet, she was sorry she'd agreed to spend the night there. She would have enjoyed leaving when Marc did, and maybe seeing him again that evening. However, instead of heading toward the parking lot and his truck, he came along beside them in the direction of the chalets.

"I'm parked over in the campground," he said. "Could I invite you to dinner?"

"Hey! Yeah! Mom, that's great! Let's go," said Jason with his usual enthusiasm. "You know you're always too tired to cook after skiing all day. What are you making, Marc?"

"It's already made. A big pot of stew simmering in my slow-cooker. I plugged it in as soon as I got parked. Okay, Sharon? Better than keeping these hungry kids waiting while you get something ready."

"I'd planned on wieners and beans," she said, and Jason made a rude, gagging sound that earned him a stern look.

"And as well as cookies, I must admit I make probably the best baking-powder biscuits this side of the Rockies," Marc added.

That decided her. "Great. Sounds wonderful. But we'll bring dessert. What time would you like us there?"

"Just as soon as you're ready. I'm in about the third row back, about . . . say . . . fourth or fifth vehicle along."

"I'll find you," she said dryly. "I know those rust spots intimately."

The look he gave her suggested that he'd like for her to know more than his rust spots intimately, but after a moment he turned and skied away toward the campsite.

A long, hot shower revived Sharon enough to make the hike to the campsite without too much trouble, and Marc opened the door quickly to her knock. With four bodies inside it was cramped in the camper, but it was warm and snug and the stew and biscuits were as good as he'd promised.

"Stew?" she said, taking an appreciative bite. "I'd call this burgundy beef and serve it for company."

"That's what I'm doing," he said. "Very special company."

As delicious as the meal was, jammed into the booth around the small table, with Marc's warm thigh pressed against hers, Sharon had to force herself to concentrate on her food, on the flavors and textures in her mouth, and try to ignore the other sensations coursing through her body.

For dessert, she'd taken Zinnie at her word and raided the freezer, coming up with a homemade apple pie that had only to be warmed in the oven after the biscuits had come out. Its spicy goodness filled the small camper with a wonderful aroma, and they all ate until they were stuffed.

"I don't know if I can hold this," she said when Marc set a big mug of hot chocolate in front of her.

He slid in beside her again and looked into her eyes. *I could hold you*, they seemed to say, and she shifted an inch or two away, crowding into Roxy, who said, "Mom, can I be excused, please?"

Sharon laughed. "Well, sure you can, honey, but I don't see where you're going to go."

"Up there. Jason and I can go up there and read our comics, can't we? I've finished my chocolate."

"Up there" was the double berth over the cab of the truck, and it was Marc who gave permission. Eagerly, the kids scrambled up. Marc leaned in and turned on a light at one end of the bunk. He was good with kids. She had to hand him that.

Sharon felt more relaxed now that she didn't have to touch Marc, and finished her chocolate leisurely.

"You cooked, I'll clean up."

"You wash, I'll dry. I know where everything goes."

She nodded. "In a space like this, I guess everything has to go in exactly the right spot."

They worked together harmoniously, bumping into each other now and then, but there didn't seem to be anything threatening in those gentle touches. They had just finished when Jason said, "Mom, Roxy's asleep."

She pulled a face. "I was afraid of that. Oh, well, I can stuff her into her outdoor clothes and carry her."

"No you won't," Marc said. Quickly, he got into his own boots and jacket, found a thick blanket, took it up to the front of the camper, and wrapped the sleeping child in it carefully. "You carry her things, and I'll carry her."

"You do that very well," she whispered, as he rolled Roxy out of the blanket onto her bed without disturbing her.

"I had some practice once," he said, reminding her with a sharp pang that he'd been a father and a husband at some time in his life, way back in that past that she knew held the answers to what made Marc Duval the kind of man he was, a drifter with callused hands and smooth manners.

He stood nearby while she tucked her daughter warmly into the bunk in the loft where the children were to sleep. Back downstairs, she found Jason nearly dozing on the couch by the fire. "Up to bed with you, too, my love, if you want some energy to ski tomorrow."

He didn't even try to argue, just said good night to Marc and climbed the stairs, weariness in every step.

Marc sat looking at her for a long moment, and when he stood, she did the same. They met in the middle of the room, and she walked into his arms as if it had been predestined from the moment they met at the foot of the slopes. They stood not moving, not speaking, just absorbing each other's warmth, each other's scent, her cheek on his chest, his on the top of her head. "Sharon," he said finally, sliding his hands into her hair. "Lord, just to hold you without your fighting it is heaven, but I want to kiss you too."

"Yes," she said, her hands going around his neck, fingers threading through the hair that hung down over his collar. She lifted her face, a smile on her lips. "Kiss me, Marc."

It was a gentle kiss, with none of the boiling urgency that had driven them before. This was a kiss of exploration, slow and sweet and almost numbing to her senses. He moved his lips from hers, tracing a line along her jaw with his tongue. She shuddered as a sharp knife of delight stabbed at her, and felt the sucking of his lips against her skin, the nip of his teeth, the kiss to soothe the tiny sting, and shivered again.

She arched, giving him more access, and sighed with a tremulous sound that made him hurt wonderfully somewhere deep inside.

He slid his hands under her sweater and felt her gasp of pleasure when he found her nipples under the silky fabric of a teddy. "Marc . . ." Her soft whisper held sheer bliss as she moved against him, accepting his touch with such open yearning that his intentions to move slowly, cautiously, were nearly turned to smoke.

"Yes, I know," he murmured. "It feels good, doesn't it?"

"I can't tell you . . ."

"You don't have to. It feels the same to me. Lord, but I'd like to make love to you tonight, my angel."

"Oh, Marc!" She could feel his arousal hard against her stomach, and she wanted to reach down between them, caress him as he was touching her. But she knew what he was saying, agreed with it even while her body cried out that to deny themselves was insane. "I don't remember ever wanting anything as badly as I want that, but . . ."

"I know." He lifted his head, cradled hers between his hands, and looked into her eyes. "We aren't in any hurry," he said reassuringly. "We can wait. We can have this in the meantime." He joined their mouths again and lifted her sweater. Bending, he took one hard nipple into his mouth along with the soft cloth of her pink teddy.

She looked down at him, at his dark-gold hair, his gold-tipped lashes, his closed eyes. His face had the look of a man at peace as he suckled her.

Slowly, her knees gave way, and he caught her, lowering her to the hearth rug.

Then, with a sigh of regret, he lifted his head and pulled her sweater back down reluctantly, as if putting temptation out of reach. "I have to stop now," he whispered. "I have to, or . . ."

"Yes. Please stop," she said, sitting up, drawing her knees to her chest and wrapping her arms around them. "And make me stop, Marc. My kids are just up there." She glanced at the open loft above them. "I know as well as you do that we can't."

"We will, though," he said with confidence, smoothing her hair back from her face. "I promise you, we will."

She nodded, but tentatively. As hard as waiting was, as much as she ached to join her body with his, rushing this incredible thing that was growing between them would be wrong. And it wasn't just that her kids were upstairs. There were other bedrooms, any one of which they could have disappeared into. But she knew she couldn't, not now while she still lacked trust, still lacked the ability to believe in him.

She stared at the flames behind the glass door of the airtight stove and wondered if that trust would ever come. So much had happened to her, so many hurts, such a great deal of pain. Could she rise above that and accept what this man offered, as limited as it might be?

Until she knew that about herself, she knew she couldn't accept the pleasures they could generate together. This time, she had to be certain. A small voice reminded her that she had been certain with Ellis, but she argued back that then she had been young, inexperienced.

And yet, how experienced was she now? She

had known one man in her life. Ellis. What kind of man was he to base all her decisions upon? The question she had to ask was what kind of a man was Marc Duval?

As he stood and drew her up into the loose circle of his arms, gazing into her eyes with a depth of understanding and longing that stunned her, she knew she was in deeper trouble than she had ever thought. Dimly came the tinkle of golden bangles. Oh, yes, Grandma Margaret had struck again. Sharon just hoped she knew what she was doing.

"Good night, sweet Sharon," he said, placing a tiny kiss on her nose.

"Will you come for breakfast?" she asked, feeling suddenly shy and awkward. What if Grandma Margaret's magic wasn't as potent as she thought it was? What if Marc was leaving now because he really didn't want her all that badly? He could have pushed. One more kiss, another few strokes of his tongue over her rigid nipples, and the overture would have finished; it would have been time for the full symphony to begin. She had been ripe for seduction, and yet . . . he was leaving. Could he, somehow, sense her inadequacy? "The . . . the kids would like it."

"Would you?" He smiled, his golden eyes agleam with a tenderness that shook her deeply.

She nodded. "Yes. I'd like it too."

"That's what counts with me. I'll be here."

"Okay. See you. Good night."

Suddenly, he snatched her into his arms and kissed her with such force that it drove her head back. She clung to him, her fingers digging into his shoulders as if she couldn't bear to let him go.

"Oh, Lord!" he moaned, lifting his head and

setting her away from him. "I must be out of my mind!"

She knew she was, as she watched him close the door behind him, because suddenly she recognized him for the kind of man he really was: He was the one man in the world who could do what Ellis, for all his cruelty, had failed to do. He was the man who could destroy her utterly.

Five

"Hi everybod—Marc! What a treat!" As Zinnie opened the door to the chalet, she came to a halt, arms laden with bags that Marc leaped up to take. "So Sharon invited you along too. What a great idea."

"No," he said, setting the bags down on the counter near the stove. "I invited myself along. I saw her and the kids loading up their car and decided that this was likely where they were headed. I've got my camper set up over in the campgrounds. They invited me for breakfast, though. We're running late this morning. I guess we were all tired after yesterday's skiing. Uh, is Harry out there with more stuff to bring in?"

At Zinnie's nod, he stuffed his feet into his boots and went out, leaving Sharon feeling as if he'd deserted her, left her open to an interrogation.

"We had dinner in Marc's camper last night," Roxy said, hopping down from her seat at the breakfast table. "And I fell asleep on his bed. I've never eaten in a camper before or slept in one. I really, really want to go camping," she said earnestly. "Marc says sometimes you can even feed squirrels right at your picnic table."

"Well, maybe one day you will," Zinnie told her, and then turned to pat Sharon's cheek, saying softly, "You wear such a pretty blush, my dear. Did you think I was thinking things you wouldn't want me to be thinking?"

Sharon had to laugh. "Well, actually, yes."

Zinnie's blue eyes danced with amusement. "I'd never believe such a thing about you."

That made Sharon stand back and look at the older woman questioningly. "Why not?"

"Because you told me yourself that you're too old to go looking for excitement, and I think Marc Duval is probably one of the most exciting men I've met in a long time. Not, of course, that *I'm* interested. At my age, Harry is more than enough for me." She grinned. "He always has been. I believe Marc Duval is the same kind of guy—more than enough for any woman who's lucky enough to have him, although I realize you aren't in the least bit interested in him."

Sharon put her hands on her hips. "Zinnie, why do I get the idea that you're making fun of me?"

"Because I am, silly!" Leaning closer as she dug several cans of soup out of one of the bags, she whispered, "Did you really make him spend the night alone in his camper?"

Sharon nodded, knowing her cheeks were growing hot and pink at the older woman's directness. "It was a mutual agreement. He didn't want it any other way either."

At that, Zinnie laughed. "Among all those other trades he's learned, acting must be included, if he convinced you of that. There now, hand me that other bag, and I'll get this stuff stowed too.

We're earlier than we'd expected, because we both woke up well before daylight and found ourselves itching to be on the slopes."

As she finished speaking, the men came in, both carrying suitcases and more bags of groceries.

"Looks like you're setting up for a siege," Sharon said, quickly taking the empty grocery bags from the counter to make room for the full ones. She folded one carefully, avoiding Marc's gaze as he stood nearby folding another.

"We like to eat," Harry said, taking packages of hot chocolate mix, marshmallows, and cookies from one of the bags he'd carried in. Winking at Jason, he added, "Besides, we'd hate to have the kids go hungry while we're together."

"Don't worry, Sharon. We brought lots of real food, too, so it won't be junk, junk, junk all day long."

"I wasn't worried. Your kids seemed to grow up with fairly straight bones. And their teeth look good to me."

"False teeth, both of them," said Harry. "Sad cases. Now, if we're all finished in here, how about we hit those slopes?"

While everyone else changed into ski clothes, Sharon loaded the dishwasher, turned it on, and went to wipe off the table, only to find that Marc had already done so.

"We work well together," he commented, taking the cloth from her hand and throwing it into the sink.

She murmured something noncommittal and said that she was going to go and get into her ski suit. Catching her hand, he swung her to face him, tilting her chin up with one hand. "Hey, it's okay, you know. I made sure Harry knew I'd spent the night in my own camper."

"Don't be silly. Why would you bother to do that? I have nothing to feel guilty about. Besides, we're both adults, and if we had wanted to spend the night together, it would have been our decision." She tried to pull free, but he held her fast.

"Ahh, but we *did* want to spend the night together, didn't we?"

Just thinking about it started up that deep, heavy throbbing inside her again, tightening her chest, making it difficult to breathe, let alone speak. "Marc, let me go."

His amber eyes held her gaze intently. "Answer me, first."

"No."

"No, you won't answer me, or no we didn't both want to spend the night together?"

"We made a mutual decision not to," she said, her heart's thudding making her voice vibrate. "It was the right one."

He smiled, a rueful look in his eyes. "Was it? The restless night I spent tells me different. Did you sleep well?"

She wanted to lie but knew he could see the circles under her eyes, feel the tension in her body as it quivered against him. "No," she whispered.

"Good." He let her go. "Get changed. I'll meet you over at the base of the yellow chair."

"You don't have to ski with me and the kids," she said. "You'd have more fun on the runs I can't take them on."

He chuckled. "Not a chance. You don't get away from me that easily. Where you ski, I ski." And then, with a touch that just barely grazed her cheek yet left her feeling branded, he was gone. For too many moments she stood there, breathless and giddy and inordinately happy. He really wanted to be where she was?

"Oh, go on," Zinnie said. "You deserve a break. I've been watching you ski. You're more than good enough to run the face. Take her, Marc. Let her show you what she can do. Challenge her to a race or something. Sharon, you're not a woman to turn down a challenge, are you?" Without waiting for a reply, she rushed on: "I'll come down with the kids, assuming I can keep up with them. I seem to be tiring more easily this year than ever before."

"I haven't noticed," Harry said dryly, scooping Roxy up under his arm as he backed into the chair that came to sweep them off their feet. Zinnie laughed as she aligned herself beside Jason and caught the next chair.

"A dead heat," Marc said, after their race. He was breathing heavily and shoved his headband up into the front of his hair, leaving little tufts sticking up all over the place. His face was red above his tightly curled beard and his eyes shone brightly.

"That . . . was . . . wonderful!" Sharon was puffing even harder than he as they stopped at the bottom of the steep run. "I haven't had such a good workout in ages!"

Marc smiled at her, his eyes full of admiration. "You are good," he said. "Tell me you were part of the national ski team or something. My male ego is bruised."

"And you're being kind to my female ego. I know you held back in order not to beat me."

"No way. It was a fair race, and we tied. We're very well matched, Sharon." The look he gave her was a challenge of another sort, a challenge to deny his words and the real meaning behind them.

She accepted it by speaking only to his more obvious meaning. "Hardly. You outweigh me by probably ninety pounds, are nearly a foot taller, and are a lot stronger. You could have won the race if you'd wanted to."

"You're not a modern woman who thinks that anything a man can do a woman can do just as well?"

"Of course I am, if what we're talking about is anything that takes brains. If I want muscle, I can rent a forklift."

He laughed and swung an arm around her, nearly upsetting her because she wasn't expecting it. He steadied her until she got her skis back under her securely. "Want to go again?" he asked.

"I'm game. But let's do the Westerly this time."

By the time Sharon had to leave, she was all skied out but feeling exhilarated and yet at peace. A two-day break had been just what she needed after the pressures of preparing not only for Christmas, but a wedding as well.

"I'll drive you down to the parking lot," Marc offered, after she'd kissed her kids good-bye and given them a list of instructions regarding behavior. "It'll save you lugging all your gear aboard the bus."

"No, no. I don't mind the bus. You stay and enjoy the skiing."

"Enjoy? Without you? You have to be kidding. I'm heading back now too. I just wish you didn't have your car here. Then you could ride home with me."

"Well," she said, struggling not to let her suddenly choked breathing reflect in her speech, "I do have my car, and I'm afraid I need it for work tomorrow." She was glad, though, of the ride down the steep, crooked hill to the parking area.

As he turned on the ignition, the radio came on, and he immediately switched it off with a sheepish grin in her direction. "You'd probably hate my favorite station. I'm forty-one and like golden oldies."

She turned the radio back on, saying, "And I'm thirty-seven and like golden oldies too," then proved it by singing along with the Everley Brothers. Marc joined her, and she had to smile. He did sound like an old crow!

At the bottom of the hill, Marc put her skis on top of her car for her, waited to be sure her engine was warmed up and running properly, and then said, "Okay, you lead out, I'll follow."

All the way home, she knew that those were his headlights visible in her mirror. It felt odd, being shepherded like that—odd, but sort of nice, as if she had a guardian angel on the road with her. It was not, she told herself, a feeling she wanted to get used to. She could look after herself very well indeed.

It was difficult, though, to be self-reliant, when no sooner had she pulled into her drive than he pulled into his, stepped over the low boxwood hedge that separated their driveways, and brushed her hands aside to undo the brackets that held her skis in place. He carried them and her small suitcase to the back door for her. They both heard the phone ring inside, and she gave him a wave and a mouthed "Thanks," as she unlocked the door and shoved it open.

It was Lorne Cantrell, her banker friend, on the phone. "Have dinner with me tonight, Sharon," he said.

She was surprised to hear from him. "I . . . I didn't expect you back from Disneyland so soon. What about your children? Are you sure you want me there?"

"I didn't mean here," he said. "I've made reservations at the Roost." That, she thought, was just a tad presumptuous on his part, unless he had someone else he could call if she refused, or he was willing to dine out alone. "I couldn't get hold of you all day, so I went ahead anyway, just in case you were back in time. You know what it's like there; impossible to get a table at the last minute. I've even booked a sitter for you," he added, further startling her.

"That was . . . thoughtful, but I don't need one. My kids are up at Mount Washington with friends. But are you certain you want to leave yours tonight? You don't get to spend a lot of time with them, Lorne."

"They aren't here. Marilee got sick down in California, so I brought them back and dropped them off with their mother before coming home. A sick child needs a mother, don't you agree?"

"I, well, yes. Certainly." But she didn't think it was fair to the other two to have their allotted time with their father curtailed simply because eleven-year-old Marilee was ill.

"So dine with me. Okay? I'll pick you up about seven forty-five."

She was about to refuse, to plead weariness from two days of hard skiing, but then she remembered with whom she had spent much of those two days, and what it had done to her equilibrium. She'd be better off getting away, in case she was tempted to do something stupid like go over and see if he needed any help moving his sleeping bag into the house.

"Fine. Thanks, I'll be ready."

When a knock came at the door, she thought Lorne had arrived an hour early. She was nowhere near ready, having just come out of the shower.

It was Marc, though. A smile creased his face as his eyes swept over her clinging yellow robe and the dripping hair peeking out from under a pink and white striped towel.

"Hi," he said. "I wondered if maybe we could find someplace nice and go out for dinner together."

The look in his eyes and the flutter in her stomach made her doubly glad she was able to say, "Oh, I'm sorry, Marc. I can't. That was my friend Lorne Cantrell on the phone. I've already agreed to have dinner with him."

"I . . . see." She watched his Adam's apple bounce up and down, and then he shrugged. "All right, then. Another time?"

"Thank you. Maybe."

"Well, good night, Sharon. Enjoy your dinner."

"Thanks. I imagine I will. The food at the Roost is normally very good. We go there a lot, Lorne and I. We have reservations there for the New Year's Eve dinner-dance too," she felt compelled to add. Marc Duval and the things he did to her had to be held at bay. One way or another, she was bound to make sure of that, even if it meant throwing Lorne in his face and pretending that her relationship with the banker was more important to her than it really was. It was the only safe way.

Before she had been at the table long enough to finish one drink, Sharon realized Lorne Cantrell was a bore. Of course, she'd known he wasn't one for scintillating conversation, and he didn't have an endless store of interesting tales to tell, but she hadn't known before just what a dull person he was. She had simply seen him as safe, and safe was what she was looking for. She had thought boring would be nice for a change. It was not. It was simply . . . well, boring.

However, to her dismay, Lorne made it clear over their coffee and liqueur that he wanted to take their relationship several steps further ahead than she was prepared to consider, and all of a sudden the conversation wasn't dull. It was downright horrifying.

Leaning across the table, he shoved aside the candle that separated them and took her hand. "Sharon, why don't we get married?" he said, stunning her completely.

"Lorne! We've never even been to— I mean I don't think we know each other well enough yet to make that kind of commitment."

"We've never been to bed together," he said, finishing the sentence she hadn't, "because you've always kept up a barrier between us. But I realized on this trip with the kids that I can't do it all alone any longer. I mean, well, Marilee didn't exactly get sick." He grimaced. "She, uh, got her period for the first time. Really, Sharon, it was a terrible time for me," he added earnestly, a frown on his long face. "It just blew me away! I wasn't prepared to deal with something like that! I got a hotel chambermaid to come in and help her, and then we caught the next flight back. It was no fun, let me tell you." He shoved his hair back in an uncharacteristically nervous gesture, and she couldn't help but notice that he quickly drew it forward again to cover his growing bald spot.

"And Heather is nearly ten," he went on. "It's going to happen to her too. Thank goodness Phil won't pull a lousy stunt like that on me."

Sharon had the feeling that Lorne had been more concerned with his own feelings than those of his likely frightened daughter.

He seemed to blame his daughter for something over which she had no control. She hoped he hadn't made poor Marilee feel dirty or guilty or ashamed, that he'd had the sensitivity not to let his own obvious repugnance show, but suspected that he probably had made his daughter feel worse. She could only hope that the girl's mother had taken up the slack when the kids were dropped off on her several days before their vacation was supposed to end.

"So you see what I'm saying, don't you? If you and I were married, then when the kids are with me, and something like that came up, you could handle it. I mean, women are so much better at things like that than men are. Not unnaturally," he added with a short laugh. "And your boy is going to need some questions answered in a couple of years, questions I'll be able to handle a lot better than you will."

She stared at him. "You want us to get married so we can see each other's children through puberty?"

He squirmed uncomfortably and glanced around to make sure no one had heard her. After all, it wouldn't do for one of the town's leading bank managers to be overheard discussing such a thing in public.

"Well, that's only part of it. Neither of us is getting any younger, you know. Why should we spend the rest of our lives alone just because we both failed at marriage the first time? I mean, your looks won't last forever. How many more chances do you think you'll get?"

"My looks," she said, not making any attempt to hide her annoyance, "seem to be holding up fairly well, Lorne. At least, I haven't heard any complaints lately." She wondered if he knew how ridiculous he looked with his hair combed over from a part way down by his left ear? Who was he to talk?

"All right. You look great. You always do," he said, clearly knowing he was blowing it but not quite knowing how or why. "But I still think it would be a wise move for both of us to merge our families and resources."

"You make it sound like a bank transfer," she said. "Taking funds from one account and putting them into another because of higher yield, or something."

"Well, I'm sorry, but that's the way my mind works. I'm a practical man, Sharon. I've never pretended to be anything else. However, I can see that you need some time to think it all over before you agree with me that it would be the best move for both of us, and for our children."

"Lorne . . ." How could she tactfully say that she knew now beyond a shadow of doubt that she could never marry him, not for any reason in the world. She didn't even know why she had ever thought she might be able to, that there could be any benefit in it for her. There was no tactful way to say it. She opened her mouth to give him a very blunt no, but he held up a hand, stopping her word.

"No. Don't say anything. Wait. We'll see each other again New Year's Eve. You can give me your answer then."

"I can give it to you now," she said. "Maybe you could find someone else for New Year's Eve."

His pale blue eyes looked horrified. "No, I couldn't! It's much too late for that, and I've spent a lot of money on the tickets, Sharon. I can't believe you'd back out at this late date. Really, I think you at least owe me the courtesy of attending the dinner-dance with me, and waiting until then to give me your answer. I know you're planning to turn me down. I'm just hoping that you'll change your mind over the next few days, after you think about it, see the advantages our marriage would offer you as well as me."

With a little nod, he stood, picked up the check, and then held her coat for her. They drove home in silence, but when he had walked her to her door, he bent and kissed her briefly. It was a dry, emotionless little touching of lips that did nothing to make her insides quiver. Nothing. It stirred no feelings at all beyond a faint distaste.

She sighed quietly. "Good night, Lorne."

"Good night." He looked totally miserable. "New Year's Eve. Remember. Promise me that much, anyway."

She was sorry she had to disappoint him. She knew she wasn't hurting him, but she was certainly disappointing him. "Yes. Of course. I won't let you down. I'll keep our date."

She changed from her dress into a short pink wraparound robe sashed at the waist, switched on the bedside lamp, and turned the covers back, then looked at her book lying there, its cover glossy and suggestive, but its contents pale by comparison to the thoughts that kept running through her mind. No, she was in no rush to go to bed. She wouldn't sleep. She had far too much to think about, and it was early yet. In the kitchen, she turned on the light, put the kettle on, and made herself a cup of tea.

What a strange proposal that had been, not at all what she had thought Lorne would say if he ever asked her to marry him. And her response had not exactly been what she had anticipated either. She had thought that as time passed they would grow slowly closer together, and they would realize that they could have a warm and comfortable relationship as a married couple. However, maybe warm and comfortable weren't what she really wanted.

When the gentle rapping came on her back door, her heart stopped, and she set her cup down with a clatter. Standing, she found her knees would barely support her. She knew who was there, and she knew why he had come. She stepped to the door and opened it, watching Marc's expression as his gaze swept over her brief satin robe, her bare legs and feet, then back up to lock with hers.

He didn't smile, and she noticed dimly that there were lines of tension drawn from his nose to his mouth. He had changed out of his suit and tie, was wearing a flannel shirt, tight jeans, and grubby sneakers. He looked so virile, she thought briefly of slamming the door and running for her life, but knew it was ages too late for that. She stood there, lost in his gaze. She felt a newfound confidence in herself that she'd lacked before, a sureness of her own ability to cope with whatever came of this attraction she and Marc had for each other, one she had been fighting for months. Now, she no longer wanted to fight it. She just wanted . . . him.

His gaze never strayed from hers, yet she felt he was totally aware of her naked body under her robe.

"He didn't come in," Marc said finally. His voice was taut, low, throaty.

"He wasn't invited." Hers was thin and breathless.

There was a pause. Again, she watched his Adam's apple move in his throat. "Am I?"

After only a brief hesitation, she stepped back, giving him room to enter. As he kicked the door shut behind him, he reached out and gathered her close, holding her fully against him. He groaned, a deep sound of satisfaction, pulling her closer. She sighed, a long, tremulous sound of rapture, and burrowed into his incredible heat.

No, warm and comfortable she would wait for. Those were for when she was old. Right now, she could do with a whole lot of hot and wild and exciting. Right now, she could do with a whole lot of Marc Duval, and the devil with the consequences. Lifting her hands, she drew his face down and parted her lips as his covered them.

Moments later, he lifted his head and whispered, "What's the matter? Didn't he buy you dessert? You still seem mighty hungry."

"I didn't want the kind he was offering."

"Do you want what I'm offering?"

"How do I know, until you tell me what it is?"

He bent and murmured in her ear, his words so erotic they made her squirm, and she knew her face was aflame even as she looked at him. "I want what you're offering. Oh, Marc! I want it so bad!" she said tremulously.

Lifting her in his arms, he held her high against his chest, and finally, he smiled. "Then come and get it, little one. I'm hungry too."

Something jangled musically just at the periphery of her hearing as he swung her around and carried her toward the stairs, and into her mind floated the image of golden bangles sliding along a dark, slender arm as it lifted to encircle a man's neck. *Yes*, she said silently and with gratitude. *Oh, yes. Now I understand!*

Six

He paused halfway up the stairs to kiss her again, as if he couldn't wait another moment. He set her on her feet in the upstairs hallway, holding her when she swayed. "Where?" he asked, his voice tight. He cleared his throat and laughed. "Look what you've done to me. I can hardly talk."

"In here." He thought he could hardly talk? She could hardly walk! With their arms around each other, they walked the few feet necessary into her room. Her double bed, top sheet already turned back, stood in the middle of the room invitingly, the one lamp casting a glow across a pillow where she had left her book.

He didn't move toward the bed, though, only drew her close and slid his hands into her hair, looking deeply into her eyes. "Do you always read in bed?"

She nodded, unable to speak.

"Not tonight," he whispered.

She shook her head.

"I like your room. It smells like you, sweet and delicate, like a field of wildflowers. And it looks like you, all neat and tidy and dainty. Do you know, it scares me how small you are. I'm not so sure I won't hurt you if I love you the way I want to—hard and fast and furious until there's nothing left of this vast need in me." He smiled. "As if that could ever happen. Because even if I did love you that way, I know I'll always want more."

"I'm like a reed," she said huskily, lifting a shaking hand to stroke the soft beard as it curved around under his chin. "I'll bend. So hold me tight, love me the way you want to. The way I want you to."

But when he lifted her and laid her on the bed, parted the front of her pink robe, and curved his hands around her creamy breasts, she shivered and couldn't continue to meet his gaze.

His hands moved to her shoulders. "What's wrong?"

She had to tell him! She gulped, closed the front of her robe, and said, "Marc . . . You have to know something about me. I'm . . . not very good at this. I don't . . . I haven't . . . Not for a long time and . . ."

He lay down beside her, turned her face to his, forcing her to meet the ardor in his dark gold eyes. "How long, sweetheart?"

He had misunderstood. She knew that and was suddenly glad. Maybe he'd never known a woman like her before, a woman who was unable to function normally in a sexual situation. "Dysfunctional" was the term she had read more than once in self-help articles. Once, she had been extremely . . . functional. But that enjoyment had died a long time ago along with many other good things she had once known.

"Three years," she said, answering the question she knew he was asking. It had been three years since she had had sex. It had, however, been much, much longer since a man had made love to her.

"I will have to be very, very careful with you," he said. "Never do I want to cause you a moment's pain."

"What about the pain of waiting?" she asked, lifting up on one elbow, beginning to unbutton his shirt. If she was going to do this, she had to do it now. Right now.

His chest was liberally covered with the softest, curliest mat of hair she had ever seen, paler than his beard, but nearly as thick. She ran her hand into it, curling her fingers to press their pads against his hard muscles.

His chuckle sounded against her neck as he nuzzled her skin. "That kind of pain," he said, "is good for you."

"And for you?" She found his nipples and squeezed them gently in turn, then kissed one, washing it with her tongue. He went very still, just holding her face to him with one hand on the back of her head.

Several moments later he said hoarsely, "I don't think that kind of pain is good for me. I might have a heart attack."

She lifted her head, eyes filled with alarm. "You have a bad heart?"

Stroking one hand up over her bent knee and down the slope of her thigh, he pushed the back of her satin robe up until he found warm, rounded flesh to touch, and the edge of a pair of panties. One finger slipped under the elastic, moving erotically from side to side over the curve of her buttock. "No. But it's sure as hell racing like mad right now."

"Aerobic," she murmured, moving against him,

rubbing her cheek on his woolly chest. "Good for you."

"Oh, Lord!" He picked her up, parting her legs and sitting her astride him, nuzzling open the front of her robe. He licked the underside of one of her breasts, then pulled the tight nipple into his mouth, rubbing it with his tongue until she moaned. Still, she felt exposed sitting on his stomach, the evidence of his arousal hard under her. And the light! The light bothered her terribly. He would see. He would know. He would despise her.

"I want to lie down," she said. "Please, Marc. I can't touch you when we're like this."

"You're touching me, all right." Clasping her hips, he moved her up and down against the bare skin of his abdomen.

"Not enough," she said with a gasp. "It's not enough!"

"It will never be enough," he said, rolling her off him, lifting up to lean over her, his broad, callused hands sliding slowly up her body.

The room was plunged into darkness as she reached over and switched off the lamp.

"Why did you do that?" he murmured. "I want to see you, Sharon. Don't you know how lovely you are? It excites me just looking at you." He rolled to one side as if to turn it on again, but she caught him, held his arm in both hands, and shook her head.

"No. Please." He gave in. She fumbled with the button at the top of his jeans, popped it free, and then slid down his zipper.

"That," he said, "has got to be the sexiest sound in the world. A zipper in the dark." As her hand slipped inside the denim, he didn't speak anymore, just sucked in a sharp breath and lifted his hips up as her fingers encircled him firmly, her hand moving rhythmically. He groaned and fell back, his shirt draping open, and she moved her mouth over his chest until she found one of his nipples again and tugged on it with the same rhythm. He whispered her name in a tense voice, with a warning in his tone, but she didn't stop. His breath rasped in and out harshly.

"That," she corrected him, "is the sexiest sound in the world."

"Oh, Lord!" he said again, tearing himself from her hands and mouth, flipping her onto her back and cupping her breasts. "You want sexy sounds, woman? Then listen to yourself!"

He kissed his way from her breasts to her toes and back up again, pausing here and there until she whimpered with need and writhed on the bed. He grasped the elastic of her bikini panties and slid them off her with her full cooperation, then quickly got rid of his own clothing. His hot tongue found the pulsating center of her, and the sounds that issued from her throat made him murmur in approval. Lifting her hips, he held her to his mouth, keeping her in place when her involuntary motions would have snatched her away from the very source of her pleasure.

"Marc . . . please . . . stop . . ." She moaned, her fingers clutching his hair tightly. "I can't . . . do this. That's what I was trying to tell you. I haven't . . . had an orgasm for a long time. I can't!"

He lifted his head long enough to gasp, "You can, you will, you are," and continued his sensual caresses, until suddenly, she knew he was right. She squeezed her eyes shut as she soared up, up, up, went rigid, striving for something just out of reach. When she found it, she let out a glad cry, trembling and sobbing as he rested his head on her heaving abdomen.

"Sexy sounds," he murmured as she stroked his hair, her fingers still shaking. "Such beautiful music, my Sharon. I want you to sing for me like that again and again."

He nestled her close in his arms, licking the salty tears from her face. "I've been empty for so long," she whispered. "I know I shouldn't feel that way, but I do. I need you again, Marc. I need you inside me."

"Yes." He rolled away from her, and she knew he was preparing himself. She rested her cheek against his back, running her hands around his waist. She quivered, a deep shudder of need frightening her once more with its intensity, because what if she couldn't find that wonderful place again, the way normal women did? What if what had just happened was a fluke? And then he turned, cuddling her close again. She could almost believe that it would be all right. Yet there was still that element of doubt, of fear, and she had to know!

"Please . . . I want you to hurry now," she said, but he still held back. Parting her legs, he probed with one finger, finding hot, satiny moisture, and slipped inside her, parting her, widening the entrance, working in and out. She gasped, writhed, and dragged him to her. "Now!" she said, but he still resisted.

"Let me turn on the light," he said thickly. "I want to see your face. I want to see what we look like together. Please, Sharon."

Her robe was undone, but it still covered her back, and she was afraid if she didn't do what he said he would leave her like that, hung up on the edge with nowhere to go. She was aching with need, burning with it, had no one but him on her mind. The rest didn't matter as much as what she needed at that moment.

"Yes, yes, anything, just don't stop . . . Oh, Lord, Marc, promise me you won't let it stop this time!" she cried softly.

The light wasn't bright, but she squeezed her lids down tightly nonetheless. She knew he was looking at her; she could feel his gaze sweeping over her body. When he whispered to her to open her eyes, she forced herself to obey, staring into the tawny depths of his.

"I love you, Sharon." He said it quietly but with deep conviction. She wanted to reply, to tell him the same, but her throat was filled with an aching tightness she couldn't swallow, so she could only look at him and hope he understood.

He moved over her, then took her slowly, inch by inch, letting her get used to the feel of him inside her. All the while he gazed at her face, his own a taut mask of control. When he was as deep inside her as he could go, he stayed very still for several beats, then withdrew until her clenching muscles and the alarm in her eyes drew him back. He thrust again, one rushing plunge after another as she cried out. Her legs wrapped around him, her nails raked his back, her body arched into a taut bow as she reached ever higher until she was *there* again. The sensation was upon her in such a rush she had no control over it, had to go with it, let it take her where it would. Dimly she was aware of the same thing happening to Marc, and she held him with a fierceness she had never known before, helping him over the edge.

"How can so much woman be packaged in such a petite body?" he asked sometime later, and she had to smile at the way he pronounced "petite"—

perfectly, not the way it was said in the English language. He gave it special charm, and she had a dim memory of his having murmured more French words as they'd made love.

She didn't say anything. There was nothing she could say. She could only lie there in his arms and savor the feelings seeping through her. She had made it. Twice, she had made it. She wasn't what she had thought for so long. She wasn't what Ellis had told her she was. It wasn't the euphoria of elation she felt, she decided, examining her emotions, it was the quiet joy of personal vindication. She wasn't "frigid." She wasn't "sexually dysfunctional" as the magazine articles had so tactfully put it. She was whole. She was normal. She was a woman!

"What are those for?" Marc kissed the tears from her cheeks.

"I don't know. Happiness, maybe."

"I hope so, Sharon. Because you've made me very happy. Happier than I've been for a long time."

"That's the way I feel." Shyly, she looked at him through her black lashes. "I didn't know I could . . . do that . . . anymore."

"Do what?"

She felt a flush rising on her face. Dammit, she was thirty-seven years old. She was the mother of two children! She could certainly tell this man who had just become her lover her innermost thoughts, couldn't she? "I didn't know I could reach a climax."

"So you said earlier." He smiled slowly, sexily, making her want him all over again. "I don't know why you would think that," he said. "You're a very responsive, sensuous woman. Any man would know that, looking at the clothes you wear." He fingered the satiny fabric of her robe. "Things like this, like the velvet and fur of your bridesmaid's gown, the silk dress you wore Christmas Day, like the velour thing you had on when I came to ask you out for dinner. You like soft, you like smooth . . . and so do I." His gaze held hers, mesmerically. His hands slid the robe down off her shoulders, over her arms. "Your skin is the smoothest . . . the softest, the most touchable skin in the world." Lifting her unresisting body, he sat her up and slipped the robe right off her, sliding his hands up and down her back.

Suddenly his hands stopped, one returning to a certain spot, his fingertips touching something. He felt her go rigid against him, and she struggled to get away, to pull her robe back up, but he carefully flipped her onto her stomach, and stared at the marks on her back.

Her entire body heaved in an attempt to get away as she cried, "Don't look at me! Stop it, Marc! Oh, Lord, please stop it!" But his gentle fingertip continued to trace the three small, round, puckered scars, all the more horrible as he realized what they were—cigarette burns.

All at once, he thrust himself away from her. She heard his feet thudding on the carpet, heard the bathroom door open and close with a bang that shook the house. She pulled her robe back on, covering her shame, and huddled there weeping. Of course he would despise her now. How could he help it? He knew what she had allowed Ellis to do to her. He knew she was weak and ineffectual and useless as a woman, as a human being. The good effects of more than two years of counseling faded away. She wanted to die right there, but it came at her in waves as she curled into a fetal position and stopped trying to fight it. Marc had seen. He knew. And he had left her.

Marc felt ill. He leaned on the basin with both hands and retched dryly. Sharon had been physically as well as emotionally abused! He remembered her saying that her divorce had meant the end of pain. And he thought she meant unhappiness. Oh, Lord, how could she ever have trusted a man to come near her again? How had she ever managed to trust *him*? He groaned as he pounded his fists on the edge of the basin, fighting against the anguish that tore into him.

He loved her! He wanted to make a future with her, but she had been abused, scarred inside and out, injured by the man she loved! Of all the men for her to turn to, it should never have been him! Once she knew the truth, the trust would die. And when it did, that tiny, glowing brightness he had sensed still lived inside her somewhere wouldn't burst into flames of love for him as he had been praying it would.

What he should do was get his clothes on, leave her house, get into his camper, and drive away. But where could he go? He wasn't ready to go home. He had been so sure that he had found the place for him, the place where he could make a new life, be truly happy again.

But not without Sharon. He knew that now. Without her, he would never be happy no matter where he went.

He heard the door open and looked up, staring at the ghostlike little figure that came through. Her face stark white between the black brackets of her hair. She held his clothing in one arm.

In a tiny, frightened voice, she said, "I brought your things. Good-bye, Marc. I'm . . . sorry."

He stared at her, his mouth in a hard, set line. "Why?" he croaked. "Why the hell did he do that to you?"

His fist hammered on the edge of the basin, and she recognized the muffled sound that had made her hesitate outside the bathroom door for so long. The violence of it terrified her even further, and she backed up, out the door. He followed her, as she crowded away from him, her gaze never leaving his face. "No," she whispered. "Please don't be mad at me. I won't let it happen again. I didn't mean to upset you. I—" She gasped as his hands clamped down on her shoulders.

At once, he let her go, lifting a gentle hand to touch her cheek, shoving her hair back. He remembered how she had had the same haunted, stricken look on her face outside his camper on Christmas Eve. He'd been confused by that diffidence following each little spurt of entirely forgivable temper, but now he thought he understood it.

"Sharon." He swallowed as he lifted her face and looked into her terror-filled eyes. "Don't be afraid of me. Please, *ma chérie*, no fear. I will not 'urt you. You haven't upset me. I was upset by what I saw 'ad been done to you, but I'm not angry wit' you. How could I be? You are too precious ever to be harmed in any way."

His quiet voice was calming, and his accent more pronounced. Oddly, that helped the fear begin to abate, as if some part of her knew that he was speaking from the heart, not taking care with his pronunciation as he usually did. But she still eyed him warily, still kept her back pressed into the corner in case the sight of it set him off again.

It was, he thought, as if she didn't fully trust him not to turn on her in the next instant. He felt sick to his stomach, knowing his fury at what had been done to her had probably hurt and frightened her almost as much as the original abuse had. He told himself he should leave, that it would be best for her if he did. But how could he leave her like that? He had to make it up to her, calm her, get her back to her bed where she would be warm and safe.

"I just want to 'old you," he said, stroking her face again. "I want you back in my arms, trusting me." *Trust?* The word had a bitter taste in his mouth. Soon, all too soon he would have to tell her about his past, and then she wouldn't trust him to change her tire! "You thought I left your bed because I was disgusted by what I saw, yes?"

She nodded, her eyes huge and dark and fathomless.

"I was, little Sharon, but not with you," he said tenderly. "Never with you. With the monster who did that to you. Will you come back to me? Will you let me hold you? Will you give me that much trust?"

After several moments, she moved forward, and he held her loosely, stroking her hair, kissing her eyelids and her cheeks. "I'm going to pick you up now," he said, giving her plenty of time to object. She rested her cheek against his chest, but for all the trusting gesture, he felt her quivering and lifted her with great care. Carrying her back to the bed, he laid her down on it, drawing the covers up over her.

"I'm sorry I frightened you, little one. I'll leave now," he said, and turned out the light.

Out of the darkness came her faint whisper. "No. Marc, please don't go."

"You want me to stay?"

"I want you to . . . hold me."

He could see those big eyes looking at him in the light coming through the crack where he hadn't fully shut the bathroom door. It was wrong, so wrong of him not to tell her, not to give her a decent chance to make an informed choice, but he wanted so badly to hold her, too, that he couldn't resist the pleading he saw there in her eyes. He slid under the covers and felt her shivering with cold and tension.

Turning half toward her, making a little hollow in his shoulder for her head, he drew her into his warmth and pulled the covers around them both.

"Why?" he said. "Why did he do it? It was your husband, wasn't it?"

She sighed, and he didn't think she was going to tell him. But then she said, "Because I got pregnant with Roxy and wouldn't . . . do anything about it."

"Bastard!" He went rigid with fury, but felt her quiver again and knew he would have to curb any tendency he might have toward violence. Until he'd seen those scars on her back, he had never had such a tendency. It shocked him with its scope and fury. "Why," he said again more gently, "why would he want you to do a thing like that?"

"Because he thought it was bad for my career." And then, as if floodgates had opened, her words spilled out. "He didn't want me to have Jason either. We just . . . argued a lot about it until it was too late. I think he sort of liked Jason, at least at first, but when I wanted to stay home with the baby, he was furious. He said he owned me, owned my name, owned my career, and I would do what he said or else."

Marc sighed heavily, his hand smoothing satin fabric over the scars he could still see, even though they were covered and her back was turned from him. He knew he would have nightmares about them. How many nightmares was he going to be forced to endure? "Or else . . . this?"

"No. No, that started later. I just did what he wanted. He was right. He did own my name, he did own my career."

"How did that happen? He was your manager as well as your husband, I take it, but how could he own your name?"

"I don't know. He just did. A lawyer confirmed it. Before Ellis was my husband he was my teacher, my mentor. He was older, and I thought very wise, the right one to steer me through the music business." She frowned. He could feel one of her eyebrows move against his shoulder. "I was twenty-three when we married, and he became my manager. In spite of the fact that I'd been on my own and raising my little sister for five years, I was a very young twenty-three, very naive. He was also a very good composer and a harpist of fair renown, and I trusted him.

"When I started to get bookings to play at concerts and with orchestras all over North America, was even offered a contract to begin recording, he grew jealous, angry with me. He told me that it was only because the classical music community needed a token woman. I was too young to realize that he was wrong, that plenty of talented women had good positions with many different symphonies, were making recordings of classical music and going on tours. He said I wasn't very good, that I had to keep working, keep trying harder until I was perfect. But everything I wrote he rejected, until I felt he was rejecting me. He took most of the music I wrote and put it away, saying it wasn't good enough yet, that when I had 'matured' he'd give it back to me to work on again. Some, he let through because other people had heard them. Those comprised the two recordings I made.

"And then I got pregnant with Roxy."

"And he hurt you and you left him," Marc said finally.

She was silent for too long. "Sharon?"

"No. No, I didn't leave him. I should have. I know that now, but he told me he was sorry, told me I had driven him to it. To make amends, he let me keep the baby."

"Was that the only time he harmed you physically?"

"It was emotional hurts he preferred to inflict," she said, and he heard the shame in her tone. "He grew angrier and angrier, because I wouldn't play anymore. I wouldn't compose. I couldn't. I didn't have it in my soul any longer. I used to try. I'd sit there at my harp for hours in the evening after the children were in bed, when he was out of the house, and try to play with joy, the way I used to. But there was no joy in me, only sadness, so I stopped.

"I know I should have left, Marc, but I was so afraid for the children, afraid he would take them away from me. You see, by then I believed he was completely powerful, that there was nothing I could do or say to change things. Unless you've lived in fear of that kind, you can never understand. I've had a wonderful therapist helping me to understand, and without her, I never would have come through this.

"But I didn't have her then. I didn't have even an ounce of courage."

Pulling himself up against the headboard, he turned to stroke her hair, rub her cold arms below the sleeve of her robe. "You don't have to go on with this, Sharon. I think I get the picture. I understand why you don't want to play. I'm just sorry I ever pressed you to do it."

She lifted her head and smiled at him. She knew neither of them was sorry he had pressed her to do the other thing she had once been so bad at. "No," she said softly. "You never really pressed me. You just . . . asked."

"And he ordered?"

"That's right."

"You said something when we were making love. You said, 'don't let it stop this time.' Was that part of what he did to you?"

She nodded, and even in the dim light, he saw color stain her cheeks. "He . . . didn't touch me, really, other than in hatred, I suppose. He would . . . seduce me, I guess is the only word for it, make me want him, and then leave me . . . unfinished. It got so I hated sex as much as I hated music, and the harder I tried to be successful with either one, the farther from it I fell. He said I had become frigid through having Roxy, that if I had done what he wanted, none of this would ever have happened. And then . . . finally, he left us. I felt nothing but pure, unadulterated relief."

"But still, you can't make yourself play?"

She shook her head, meeting his gaze in the half-light. "Oh, I *can* play. You heard me at Jeanie's wedding. I want to. It's just that I won't. I told you I wasn't a failed musician, Marc. I'm simply one who quit."

He couldn't even begin to understand. He hadn't

quit what he loved doing because he'd chosen to, but because he'd been driven to it. "Why?" he asked. "Why, when it meant so much to you?"

"It still does. I ache, sometimes, to play. But if I do, then I know I'll compose again." Her face closed up, became devoid of expression, yet taut anger strained her voice as she added, "And that, I refuse to do. I won't give him anymore of myself. Not one more thing!"

Seven

Marc pulled the covers up over her legs and drew her against his shoulder, curling an arm protectively around her. "What do you mean, give him any more of yourself? Does he want you to compose again? How can you let that prevent you?"

Almost to herself, she repeated her earlier words: "I won't give him any more. He had it all once, and he came very close to destroying it. I won't allow him to destroy me."

"How would your composing give him anything?"

"I told you. He owned me, owned my name, owned my music. He still does. The Christmas he came back—we hadn't seen him for nearly three months—he was nice at first."

She gripped his hand so tightly, he thought she might crush his bones, but he let her hold him, knowing she needed to draw on his strength for what was coming.

He didn't want her to go on, but some kind of horrified fascination made him listen. Her sentences were short and choppy, her voice jerky. "He . . . .said he was sorry he'd left, but he'd had things to work out. I knew that meant another woman. He said he still cared about me, wanted things to be right between us again. I should have known he was lying. He always lied to me, but it was Christmas, and I had been terribly lonely even though Jeanie and the children were with me. I've always wanted a complete family. I guess because I lost my parents. He . . . he was supposed to be the one to complete it. I had believed that for so long, and after we talked, I was ready to believe it again. We . . . well, we went to bed together." Her voice trembled, but she forced herself to continue.

"I tried. I really did. But I simply wasn't good enough for him, and I froze up when he started telling me what a bad lover I was. Only this time, I got mad and accused him of being a bad lover too. I knew better than to talk like that to him, but I'd had enough disappointments. He slapped me a few times, then said he wanted a divorce, that he'd never really wanted me back, he'd just been trying to soften me up, and all he'd really come for was my work. He said he might as well be paid at least a part of what I owed him, and maybe he could sell some of my compositions to somebody for a few bucks.

"I told him my music was mine and I wouldn't give it to him to finance his affair. He went to the desk where he'd locked it up, but it wasn't there. I'd found the key and moved it. Our shouting woke the kids. I could hear Roxy crying in her room. Jason came out of his. Ellis was shaking me. My face was swollen. I could hardly see, but I saw Jason try to stop him. He tried to help me. He was seven years old, Marc! He was so little, so helpless against an adult man! When Ellis dropped

Jason in the middle of the room, he asked me if I wanted him to do the same to Roxy."

She gazed at him, the tragedy of the scene etched on her face, and added in a whisper, "I gave him my music."

"Yes."

She blinked, reached up and touched his face, finding it wet. "Are you crying for me?" She sounded shocked.

"Yes."

"Please don't. It was worth the trade, believe me. He left, but he still owns my name, and anything I write, so I don't write music anymore."

"What happened then?"

"Jeanie came home from a date and found Jason and me on the floor. She called an ambulance and the police, but by the time the police went after him, Ellis had got on a plane and was in Europe. In time, our bruises healed, but Jason still has scars inside. He's never forgotten that night. For a couple of years, he didn't even like the smell of Christmas trees, but this year he didn't say anything when we put it up.

"Anyway, Ellis divorced me and married a twenty-three-year-old student of his. Two or three times a year he releases a piece of 'her' music. She's receiving quite a lot of acclaim internationally. I only hope he doesn't get jealous of that."

"*Her* music?" Her stressing of the pronoun hadn't escaped him.

She shrugged. "If it belongs to him, and it does—that's ironclad, I was told by a lawyer— then I guess he can give it to whomever he wants and call it hers. All I know is that it isn't mine, even though a bit of my soul is in each and every note."

Wrapping her in his arms, he slid them both down in the bed and covered them warmly again.

"Your lawyer or his?"

"His, but what difference does that make? A lawyer's a lawyer."

"Don't you believe that for one minute longer!" he said. "We're going to look into this business, my darling. We're going to see just how ironclad his 'ownership' of your music really is."

"No!" she said, lifting her head in alarm.

"Yes," he insisted, gently putting her head back down on his shoulder where he wanted it.

"Marc, believe me, I'm just glad to be out of that mess. I don't want to stir it up again. He might still hurt my kids or try to take them!"

"I will never let him hurt you or the children! And you won't be stirring anything up. I can do it in such a manner that he'll never guess it's being done until it's all finished and I've proven that he doesn't own much more than the hairs on his head, if that."

"How can you do that?" she asked. "Were you a private investigator in one of those lives of yours, until it wasn't fun anymore?"

He was very still for several minutes. "No, Sharon. I was a lawyer. I still am and it never stopped being 'fun.' It just stopped being . . . possible. And I was once very good at proving things about people."

"And?" she prompted.

"And now I'm going to prove to a certain lady of my acquaintance that she is anything but frigid, that she can and will have several very satisfactory climaxes before we both go to sleep."

He must have been a very good lawyer, she thought a long time later.

* * *

"Hey! Where do you think you're going?" Marc caught her and held her by one ankle, leaving her half on and half off the bed.

"I'm going to work," she said. "I have a family to feed."

He drew her slowly but inexorably back onto the bed. "How about me? I'm hungry too."

"Pooh!" she scoffed. "You've had enough to last any normal man a month!"

He grinned, clamped his hands around her bottom, and pulled her to him, showing her that he wasn't kidding, that his hungers were very tangible. That had the odd effect of triggering her appetite, too, but she braced her hands on his chest and pushed him away. He let her go reluctantly, and it was all she could do not to fall back into his arms. It was the only place she really wanted to be. Who in her right mind could choose a library over Marc Duval? she wondered.

But she resolutely turned away, went into the bathroom, and turned on the shower. She hadn't been in her right mind since he'd first parked his camper next door last August. Sliding the doors shut behind her as she stepped in, she soaped herself liberally. She had just begun to rinse when the doors opened and she was joined by a very large man with very large hands. Soon, she was covered with a slick coating of lather again.

"Marc . . ." Her voice was weak as she leaned back against him, his hardness pressing into her buttocks, his hands cupping her breasts. "I'm going to be late for work . . ."

"No," he said confidently. "This won't take long." He turned her and lifted her onto him. She flung her head back, calling his name as he drove inside her, deep and hard, moving her slowly back and forth, up and down, so that her most sensitive spot rubbed against him. She cried out once, twice, then moaned softly in repletion as she went limp in his arms. He surged into her again, a groan of pleasure wrung from his throat, a deep sound of satisfaction that thrilled her more than anything ever had before.

He let her feet drop to the bottom of the tub, reached around her, and shut off the water. "See?" he said. "That didn't take long at all, did it?"

Her day at work, however, took much longer than it should have. Never had she been so eager to leave that library. At noon, she watched the door, waiting for Marc to come through it as he had so many times before, big and broad-shouldered and bearded. And this time, when her blood raced and her temperature rose, she wouldn't bother to fight it. She wouldn't put on her tight librarian face, make her stare cool and repressing. This time, she would let him see all the delicious things he did to her, every little fantasy he had ever caused her to have.

Only he didn't come.

She sighed and went out alone for a bowl of soup and a sandwich, looking with disenchantment at the Christmas decorations on the buildings and in the cafe, thinking it was time they came down. Why did people insist on leaving them up until after New Years? A miserable drizzle fell, soaking through everything, running in rivulets across the sidewalk and filling the gutters. After what they had shared last night, to say nothing of this morning, surely he would have wanted to have lunch with her?

She pulled a face as she parked the car and wished she hadn't had to spend all that money last winter on a new roof. She'd really wanted a covered carport instead. Getting out, head ducked against the driving rain, she opened the trunk.

Juggling parcels, she fumbled to get her key in the lock, only to have the door swing open in front of her. She was greeted by warmth, good aromas, and strong arms sweeping her burdens away.

He set everything on the counter, gathered her up in his arms, and swung her around. "I missed you," he said.

She sighed. "I missed you, too, and expected you to show up at the library. I had a lonely lunch." She look aggrieved, her lower lip jutting out just a tiny bit. He bent, nibbled on it, then kissed it.

"I know what libraries are like," he said. "And the head librarian would not have appreciated the things I'd have said to you, possibly even done to you, once I had hauled you back into the obscure poetry section. So I stayed away."

She sighed again. "I noticed."

"But I'm here now," he pointed out.

"I noticed that too," she said, sliding her hands into the hair at the back of his neck. "I guess I shouldn't be surprised. It seems to me I left you here sometime about sixty-five or seventy hours ago."

"At least that," he agreed, undoing the buttons on her coat, shoving it off her shoulders, and flinging it onto the kitchen table. For a long time they stood there wrapped in each other's warmth and scent, kissing, murmuring. Then before she really noticed what he was doing, he had slid the zipper down the back of her dress and unhooked her bra.

She started to object, but he caught her mouth with his and silenced her while he took both dress and bra off her, stepping back just enough for them to fall to the floor at her feet.

She broke their lingering kiss and glanced down at the pool of clothes. "What are you doing?" She knew what he was doing. It just seemed sensible to have these things confirmed. After all, she might be wrong in her assumptions. Suddenly, she was looking at the top of his head.

"I'm undressing you." His lips moved over the taut skin on her stomach as he spoke. He had dropped to one knee and was gently pulling down her panty hose and panties. Holding on to his shoulders, she lifted first one foot, then the other, shuddering as his mouth did incredible things to the insides of her thighs. She moaned when he put one of her feet on his raised knee and clutched her bottom, tilting her pelvis upward, his breath hot, his tongue probing.

"Marc!" It was a gasp of shock and pleasure. Her fingers dug into his shoulders as she stared down at him. He was doing this to her right in her own kitchen. All her clothes were off, all the lights were on, and he was still fully dressed! "If I have to be undressed . . . so do you," she managed to say, but he shook his head.

"This is so much fun," he murmured, and continued. Her knees were wobbling, her mouth was open, and she was gasping for breath. If she let go of his shoulders she would collapse, but her hands were growing as weak as her knees.

"Marc . . . stop. I'm going to fall down!"

He stopped, lifted her, laid her on top of her coat on the table, and continued his sensual assault. "Marc!" My Lord! This is . . . ahh, so . . . wonderful, she finished in a hoarse whisper, replacing the word "depraved," which she had been going to use. She bucked and arched against his restraining hands as she climbed the high mountain and then slid down the other side. After a long moment, she smiled slowly and said, "You're really nice to come home to."

Lifting her off the table, he wrapped her coat around her and cuddled her close. "It's really nice to have someone come home to me," he said. "I like to show my appreciation."

She was thoughtful as she shoved her arms into the sleeves of her coat, then nestled back against him. "You certainly know how to go about it!" When was he going to tell her about the wife and child he had lost? She wanted to know, especially now that she had told him all the terrible parts of her past. But she hesitated to ask. What, after all, did this relationship mean to him? He had never said exactly. He'd said once that he loved her. He'd made some vague comments about the future, but that was a nebulous term which could mean anything from a few weeks or months to . . . eternity. But if he'd tried for eternity once and had it snatched from him, maybe he wasn't willing to try again.

"It was all a plot," he said. "I've been planning it all day." That wasn't quite true, he reflected. He had spent most of the day over in his own house making long-distance calls, learning much, but not enough to tell Sharon about.

He swallowed, thinking of other things he had to tell Sharon. He thought, not without pride, that he had managed to distract her quite successfully from asking the question he had been sure would be on her mind when she came through that door: *If you are still a lawyer, and it never ceased being fun, then why aren't you practicing law?* That distraction, however, had not been a calculated act on his part, but one that just flowed naturally from their first kiss after she got home.

He knew the question would come. He just didn't know how he was going to handle it when it did.

"Something in the oven smells heavenly," she said, finally pulling out of his arms and bending to gather up her abandoned clothes.

"Roast beef," he said. "This time of year, with all the turkey and leftovers, I start to crave red meat." He pounded his chest. "Red meat. Makes a *man* out of a man. Puts hair on your chest!"

"Whew!" she said. "I think I'll make you a turkey sandwich." Holding out her hand to him, she asked with what he found touching shyness and a hint of wistfulness, "Will it be ready anytime soon?"

He let her lead him toward the stairs. "No time soon at all."

She gave a happy sigh. "That's good. Because I don't think I'll be ready for it anytime soon." Neither of them were.

"Hi, Mom!" When the phone rang, she'd untangled herself from Marc and sheets and blankets, rolled over, and lifted the receiver. Jason's happy tones made her glance over at Marc and she blushed as if her son were able to see rather than just hear her.

"Hi, love. Are you having a good time?"

"Oh, yeah! *Excellent!*" He went into details about the day they'd had, and then put Roxy on. She was just as exuberantly happy about her unexpected ski vacation.

"Gramma Zinnie makes cookies as good as Marc's," she said, and indeed, it sounded as if she had a mouthful and was speaking around it.

" 'Gramma Zinnie'?"

"That's what she and Grandpa Harry want us to call them 'cause we don't have any real grandparents and they don't have any real grandkids, but when they do they're going to be our cousins and they'll be calling them that so we may as well start now and get them used to it."

Sharon was still shaking her head and trying to sort out all those pronouns, when Roxy handed the phone over to Zinnie.

"You don't mind, do you?" asked the older woman.

"No. No, Zinnie, I think it's wonderful the way you and Harry have adopted my kids. And me," she said with a lump in her throat.

"We've come to love you all," Zinnie said, sounding a bit throaty herself. "To get two daughters and two grandchildren through the marriage of one son has been the highlight of our lives. But we were wondering if you'd like to come up and join us New Year's Eve. If you left right after work, you could be here by early evening, and with the next day being a holiday, and the day after that a Sunday, you could get in a couple more days of skiing. You could also," she added slyly, "ask Marc to come along."

Sharon sighed and glanced over at Marc, who was lying with his hands behind his head, gazing at her. "Zinnie . . . I'd love to, but I can't. I have a date for New Year's Eve." She watched Marc's gaze narrow and looked quickly away from him.

"I'd break it if I could," she said to Zinnie, but mostly for Marc's benefit, "but it's one of those long-standing agreements, and I really can't get out of it."

"Oh, well. Never mind," Zinnie said brightly. "Maybe next year. Wouldn't that be fun? Jeanie and Max, Rolph and somebody, you and . . . somebody, and us and, of course, the kids."

"Yes," said Sharon sadly, watching Marc stand up and gather his clothes before going into the bathroom. "Maybe next year." They talked for a few minutes longer, while the sound of the shower pounded in her ears, then Sharon hung up. Marc came out of the bathroom, looked at her blankly, as if he'd never seen her before, and went downstairs.

She showered, changed into a comfortable caftan, and shoved her icy feet into fleece slippers. In the kitchen, Marc was carefully slicing the roast.

They said little, and ate even less, then left the table. She thought he might go home, but he followed her into the living room, sitting down well apart from her, looking into the flames of the fire.

Finally, he glanced over at her, his golden-brown eyes expressionless. "I'd have thought things had changed," he said in a flat tone. "That you'd cancel a date with another man, no matter how long ago you'd made it, under the circumstances."

"Marc . . ." She swallowed, moistened her lips. She felt sick. "I wish it could be different. But I already told Lorne that it would be our last date." She remembered suddenly that she was also supposed to tell Lorne her answer to his important question. Of course she knew what it was going to be; no amount of "thinking it over" would ever change her mind, not even if Marc Duval hadn't become her lover. "I tried to get out of it. But he reminded me that he had spent a lot of money for tickets, and . . ."

"I'll buy the damn tickets from him," Marc growled.

"I also said I wouldn't let him down." She bit her lip. "Lorne feels he has a . . . a position to uphold in the community. He considers himself one of the town's leading citizens. He makes business contacts on social occasions and, well, he'd feel that I was insulting him publicly if I appeared at that dinner-dance with another man while he stayed home. Everyone who knows him knows we're supposed to be there. Together."

"I find I don't really give a damn about Lorne Cantrell's feelings at this moment, Sharon. It's my feelings that are uppermost in my mind. And I hate the idea of my woman going out with another man, dining and dancing and kissing! I hate it!" he added vehemently, slamming his fist onto the arm of his chair, and she winced, staring at him, her eyes wide and dark.

Suddenly, his anger subsided. "Oh, hell, I'm sorry, little one." He came and knelt before her, taking her hands in his. "I didn't mean to yell at you. Please, don't look at me like that. Don't be afraid of me."

"I'm not afraid of you. I just—"

It was as if he didn't hear her, or maybe he didn't believe her. He went on, still holding her hands, running his thumbs soothingly over their backs. "I'll never hurt you, Sharon. I promise that solemnly. I am not a violent man. I'm just a man experiencing jealousy for the first time in his life."

"I'm sorry," she whispered. "I don't want to make you feel that way. I don't like hurting you, but this is something I have to do. I hate to break promises, Marc, and I did promise him, just last night, that I wouldn't let him down. Don't you think I'd rather be with you?"

He pulled her off the sofa and onto his lap, leaning back against the cushions, rocking her as if she were a hurt child, which in so many ways she was. Of course she hated to break promises; too many that had been made to her had been broken. She knew firsthand how it felt. "Yes," he said, "I think you'd rather be with me. It's okay, *ma petite*, I understand. I don't like it, and won't be happy to see you go out with him, but I won't try to stop you. You are a grown woman, and you can make your own decisions. I know this is the right one for you, or you wouldn't have made it."

She drew in a tremulous breath and let it out slowly. *I love you*, she thought, and wished she could make herself say it. He had, but she couldn't. The words were locked up inside her. And she didn't know if he'd said it because he thought he should, when he was about to make love to her for the first time, or because he really felt that way. He'd only said it once.

He had also said he might move on again come spring, so that nebulous "future" he'd mentioned might be very short. Maybe he still loved his wife. Maybe he always would. And there was still so much she didn't know about him. Why, for instance, if he had enjoyed his law practice, was he establishing himself as a cookie-maker?

She longed to ask those questions and more, but years of experience had taught her that it was best never to push a man to do anything he didn't want to do. And Marc, by his continued silence, had made it clear that he didn't want to talk about his past. She shivered, even in the warmth of his embrace, remembering the look in his eyes when he pounded his fist on the chair, the fury with which he had said those words: *I hate it!* He said he wasn't a violent man, but she knew every man had his breaking point, every man could become violent, if pushed hard enough.

She would never, never push.

Marc stood just at the door of the huge, crowded room. His eyes sought and found Sharon, a golden flame in her bridesmaid's gown, shortened now to just above her knees, where the white fur trim swirled as she danced. His throat tightened as he saw Lorne Cantrell's hand planted square in the middle of her back, against her skin bared by the vee of her dress, his other holding hers intimately close to his chest.

Drawing a deep breath, he forced himself to relax and searched the tables for his friends Candice and Norm, owners of one of the local stores that carried his line of cookies. When they'd learned he was to be alone tonight, they'd willingly offered him a seat at their table.

Of course, he'd already overheard Norm telling someone else that his brother and sister-in-law, who had intended to join them, were not going to make it. It hadn't taken much expertise to swing his subsequent conversation with Norm to the fact that he was dateless this New Year's Eve, and regretting it, wondering what might be on in town that a lonely bachelor could attend.

Candice had been delighted to welcome him too. "A stag is always great to have around," she said. "He can spell tired old husbands when they don't want to dance anymore."

He'd willingly promised to do just that, and now

he saw his friends on the dance floor. He waited until they went back to their table, then casually made his way through the crowd, wondering what Sharon's face would reveal when she finally realized he was there.

Sharon froze in mid-step as she walked back to their table with Lorne. Was she seeing things? Or was it just her imagination? But no, it was not her imagination. That was Marc, all right, dressed in the same dark gray suit he'd worn to the wedding and again on Christmas Day. As before, she couldn't help but think how marvelous he looked, how smooth, how suave, how . . . sophisticated. Like the well-off member of a prestigious law firm. . . .

Lorne took her arm, glancing at her as her steps faltered. "Are you all right?"

"Uh, yes. Fine. I . . . almost lost my shoe." She forced herself to walk on, and then experienced an indescribable stab of agony when she saw Marc take a tall, willowy blonde into his arms and dance her across the floor as the band began a slow, sensuous tune. She sat, staring straight ahead, struggling with the unfamiliar emotion eating at her. Who was that woman? Where had Marc found her at the last minute? And how had he got tickets, also at the last minute? To her knowledge, this New Year's Eve dance had been fully booked months ago!

". . . don't you agree, Sharon? Sharon?" She blinked and focused her attention on Lorne. They were alone at the table, the other two couples were on the dance floor.

"I'm sorry. I was off in a dream. What did you say, Lorne?"

He took her hand and put it on his lap under the table, leaning close to her. "What were you dreaming about? Do I dare think it was the future?"

"Lorne . . ." She could feel her color ebbing, and knew the time had come to make things clear to him.

"No, no," he said, patting her parted lips with two hushing fingers. "Don't worry. I won't embarrass you by demanding your answer now." He smiled with confidence that sent her heart plunging. "I can wait until I take you home after the dance." His smile faded, replaced by a look she had never seen in his eyes and feared now that she saw it. "On the other hand, I have to say I can scarcely wait to take you home after the dance. Your children are away . . . mine are at home with their mother where they belong, and it will be just the two of us. A wonderful way to start the New Year." Lifting her hand from his lap, he kissed her knuckles while she stared at him in total disgust. The touch of his lips made her skin crawl. What had she ever seen in this man, anyhow? Snatching her hand back, she half turned from him and saw Marc dancing by with that blonde in the flaring red dress.

Suddenly, she didn't want to be there. She wanted to go home and hide. She wanted to go home and cry. She wanted to pretend she had never met Marc Duval and wasn't sitting in an agony of pure jealousy knowing he was holding another woman in his arms. This was worse, far, far worse than the first time she had found out for sure that Ellis was cheating on her, and she had no right to feel the way she did. Marc had made no more commitment to her than she had made to him. And she was the one who had insisted on accompanying Lorne to the dance, insisted on honoring what she saw as a firm obligation. But now, she wanted it to be over.

She looked up again, and Marc was dancing by. He caught her eye, met her glance, gave her a grin that set her insides on fire, then he was gone again, turning the blonde expertly into an opening in the crowd, swinging her around so Sharon could look at her very beautiful face laughing up into his.

Eight

"Lorne, I'd like to go home now," she said when the pain in her throat permitted her to speak. She met her date's eyes squarely, partly so she wouldn't keep following Marc's progress through the room, partly in an attempt to convey her apology, her sincere regret that she was forced to refuse him and ruin an evening he'd been looking forward to. If only he had listened to her earlier in the week and not insisted on her keeping this date. "You already know what my answer is going to be, Lorne. I can't tell you how sorry I am, but—"

His jaw jutted out stubbornly. "I will not take you home now," he interrupted. "Do you want everyone to think we've had a fight? We haven't even had dinner yet, and I paid good money for the tickets, remember!"

She sighed. She did know. That had been his original argument for getting her there, after all. Did he think her memory so poor? "I don't see why I should miss a meal I've already paid for just because you're playing hard to get," he added, his face sulky, his eyes glittering with self-righteous indignation.

"I'm not playing hard to get," she said. "I'm trying to make you see the truth. I'm not the right person for you." *And you're not the right one for me*, she added silently, catching a glimpse of two laughing faces, two people having a wonderful time. Quickly, she looked away.

"How can you know that?" Lorne asked with deadly quiet, his hand imprisoning hers tightly as she tried to pull it free. "As you pointed out yourself the other night, we haven't even been to bed together. Listen to me, Sharon. I know I can make you happy. You just have to give me a chance."

"No, Lorne." Did he really believe she was simply playing hard to get? And if he did, did that mean that he believed forcing the issue would make a difference?

His pale blue eyes were angry, his mouth twisted in an ugly grimace. She knew then that he would not be taking her home. There was no way she would get into a car with a man in his mood. What she should do was get up and walk out, but the thought of the scene he might create held her pinned to her chair, and then the music ended and the others were heading back to the table.

"I could take a taxi," she said quietly, trying to rise, but he pulled her back down.

"You owe me the full evening," he said. I've spent a lot of money on you over the past six months, and I mean to collect."

What, exactly, did he mean to "collect"? She shuddered, but stayed where she was, trying to pay attention to Evelyn, the accountant at Lorne's bank, as she talked animatedly about her active two-year-old twins.

Dinner was sumptuous, but Sharon hardly tasted it. The wine was dry and crisp and plentiful, but she only sipped and set her glass down. Around her, laughter, talk, jokes, and happy people swirled, while inside her, fear coiled each time she glanced at Lorne's set face, at the determined way he chewed his food, gulped his drinks. He had paid for them. He was getting his money's worth.

And he thought she owed him something he was planning to collect!

Lord, why had she come? Why had she felt it necessary to try to appease him this way, to make her refusal as pleasant as possible? That was her biggest failing, she knew, always trying to avoid hurting people, steering a course away from unpleasantness. Not that she had expected conservative, quiet Lorne to start pouring the drinks back this way, nor had she expected that he'd take her refusal in anything but a gentlemanly manner. How little she knew him, even after all the times they'd dated. He had never given the impression of being a belligerent man, which had been one reason she'd continued to see him. He was supposed to be calm, quiet, *safe*. Of course, no issue had ever come up between them on which she'd had to cross him.

She had to escape. Somehow, she had to get out of there. If she called a cab, it could take ages to arrive. The taxi companies were always snowed under with business on New Year's Eve. She supposed she could hide out in the women's rest room after she'd made the call, but again, she was faced with the thought of an ugly scene; the possibility of a drunken Lorne pounding on the door made her feel ill.

No. There was only one thing to do. Sit through this interminable dinner, and then dance a few more times. Midnight wasn't that far off. Maybe by then Lorne's mood would have improved, though with the amount he was drinking, she doubted it. Maybe she'd get really lucky, and he'd pass out.

Dinner was cleared and the band started up again. Suddenly, before Lorne could ask her to dance, Marc was there, his hand on her shoulder. "May I?" he asked, and she nodded, relief flooding her.

"Yes," she said, and stood, moving into his arms. He pulled her close, and she knew that she never wanted to be close to anyone else, ever again.

"Velvet angel," he said, his mouth brushing the shell of her ear, his hand sliding slowly down her back. "Were you surprised to see me?"

She flicked a deep, dark glance up at his laughing eyes. " 'Surprised' isn't quite the word I'd have chosen."

He bent and brushed a kiss lightly over her lips. Suddenly, a hand descended on his shoulder. "Excuse me, but that happens to be my date you're trying to kiss, mister. I'm cutting in."

Marc saw the flare of fear in Sharon's eyes, saw the color fade from her face. "Sharon?" he asked. She glanced from one man to the other. If she refused to return to Lorne, he was just stupid enough, drunk enough, pugnacious enough to fight. And Marc's golden eyes had a hard, brassy cast to them. He was willing to take anybody on if she asked it of him.

She stepped back from him. "It's all right. I did come with him. I'll dance with him."

Marc, with a hard look at Lorne, shrugged and walked off the floor.

"Who is that guy?"

"My next-door neighbor."

"Why was he kissing you?"

"You really have no right to interrogate me," she reminded him quietly.

His hand tightened on hers. "Why was he kissing you?"

"It's New Year's Eve," she said more sharply than she'd ever spoken to Lorne. "People do that at this time of year."

"After midnight," he said sullenly. "Not before."

She was dancing with Lorne again when the countdown began, and they stopped along with everyone else. He counted loudly, waving his tall, silver hat in time to the chant. Holding a roll of serpentine streamer aloft ready to fling them at the stroke of midnight, he didn't seem to mind that he was one of the town's "leading citizens" making a complete ass of himself; but then, Sharon reflected, a good many others who saw themselves in that light were doing the same.

"Zero! Happy New Year!" The cry went up, and Lorne flung his streamers, tossed his hat into the air, then turned to swing Sharon into his arms for the first kiss of the year, only to find her wrapped securely in the arms of that big, blond, bearded fellow, and not even trying to get away.

Marc lifted his head for a fraction of a second. "Happy New Year," he said, and then he took up kissing Sharon again, oblivious of the hand shaking his shoulder, the voice shouting in his ear.

She pulled away from him a small bit, smiled dreamily and said, "Happy New Year to you too," and then returned to what was fast becoming one of her favorite pastimes, kissing Marc Duval.

Moments later, while most of the crowd around them sang "Auld Lang Syne," they were still swaying together, looking into each other's eyes, making silent and probably impossible promises, but this was New Year's Eve, and anything went. Finally, Sharon became aware that Lorne was there, teetering drunkenly, a different hat crookedly atop his head, several multicolored streamers around his neck, his proper banker's tie askew. Various shades of lipstick decorated his face.

"Excuse me," he said. "But you're kissing my date again, Mac."

"I'm kissing a woman who wants me to kiss her," said Marc, and did it once more—with feeling.

"Sharon!" This time Lorne's hand clamped on her shoulder, and he peeled her out of Marc's arms. "You owe me an explanation!"

"Yes," she said, shrugging his hands off her. "I do. And an answer. The answer, Lorne, is no. And this," she said, turning back into Marc's arms as the band struck up another slow, sweet tune, "is the explanation." Over her shoulder, she added a quiet "Good-bye."

They had danced for several minutes when Sharon suddenly remembered. "Oh, my gosh! I'm sorry. I shouldn't have done that. Will she mind?"

"Who?" He looked completely mystified.

"The blonde." Her voice was low and trembling. "Your date."

His smile was another one she knew she would treasure forever. "Ahhh, yes! The blonde. So now you know what I felt like when I knew you meant to keep your date, and again, tonight, watching you get into that geek's car all dressed up for him, not me."

"If murderous is how you felt, then, yes I know," she admitted.

"Her name is Candice Taylor. I'm here with her and her husband. Feel better?"

"Much." Beyond Marc's shoulder, she saw Lorne approaching again, trying to battle a path through the thick crowd. "Marc, I'd like very much to go home," she said. "But not with the man who brought me."

He laughed. "As if you really thought for one minute after you saw me here that you'd be going home with anyone else. We'll leave anytime you say, sweetheart. It can't be too soon for me. The way I want to celebrate New Year's Eve can't be done legally on a dance floor."

Then, before Lorne could fight his way through the crowd, Mark seemed to open a path as if by magic in the opposite direction, and the two of them had her cape and her purse and were gone long before the other man could get to her.

"You're very good at cutting swaths through crowds," she said as she leaned back in the seat of his truck, glad to be out of the noise and away from any possible repercussions that might have arisen. "In fact, you seem to be good at a lot of things, Mr. Duval."

He grinned at her, then winked. "I'm also very handy in the kitchen, if you recall." He wasn't talking about cooking.

She was glad the green glow of the dashboard lights would hide her suddenly flushed face. Would this man always be able to make her blush as well as make her heart pound simply by evoking an erotic memory?

She laughed lightly, sounding half amused, half chagrined. "You know what I've just done?"

"What have you just done?" Marc asked, taking her hand and holding it under his on the steering wheel.

"I think I've just rented my first forklift."

"Forklift?" He cut a bemused glance sideways at her.

She sighed and pulled her hand out from under his. "Yes. I was scared, Marc, scared of Lorne, scared of his drinking, his driving, and his not-so-veiled threats. So I called in some muscle. You."

He threw back his head and laughed. "I'll be your muscle any day of the week. Just turn on the key, aim me in the right direction, and I'll lift my fork at any bully who's bothering you." She smiled at him as he stopped for a red light, and he lifted a hand to slide it over her shining hair, cupping the nape of her neck.

"What's the going rate on rented muscle?" she asked.

He kissed her chin, then quickly, very quickly, her lips. The light changed. He let his foot up off the clutch and eased forward. "Sweetheart, you haven't rented me. What you've done is leased me. And I'm thinking along the lines of a long-term contract."

So was she. More than anything else, what she wanted in life was a forever contract with Marc Duval.

Marc awoke and knew at once that Sharon was gone from his side. There was an emptiness not only in the bed, but in his heart because she was absent. He listened, hearing only silence, waited several minutes in case she was just in the bath-room and would return momentarily, then got up and drew on his shorts and shirt. Opening the door, he looked out into the hall. From some-where downstairs a light shone, and he moved softly to the head of the stairs, paused, then walked down.

He came to an abrupt halt when he heard it, a faint whisper of sound, a tentative ripple of notes, as if a mouse were running along a keyboard. He waited, and it came again, this time with a hint of sureness in it, an entire bar of separate notes, each one softly enunciated, but lingering and fad-ing into the stillness of the night before the next one came. He sat down in the middle of the stair-case and listened while Sharon renewed her friendship with her harp.

It was, he thought, as if she and the instru-ment were conversing. She would ask a gentle question; the harp would respond. Then, it would lead for a moment, and she would, after a pause, come back with a contribution. It was fascinating as well as heartbreaking, because he knew that what she was doing was happening against her will. She was composing. Trying this, trying that, creating a pleasing phrase, asking the harp if it was better this way or that. In the pauses, he thought she might be writing down what they had agreed upon.

For more than an hour he sat there, until his muscles were cramped and his back ached for want of movement, but she still played. The phrases were coming with greater confidence now, seeming to pour from her, running up the scale and down, sometimes loud and exuberant like a stream down a rocky mountainside, other times soft and serene, a boat gliding across a faintly rippled ocean with just enough wind to keep the sails filled. Again and again, though, there were the questions and answers, the discussions between woman and harp, and the final decision was always pleasing to the ear.

And then, as softly as the music had begun, it faded away. Marc waited again, but there were no further sounds from below.

Getting up, he stretched and continued on down into the light, pausing at the entrance to the living room. He saw Sharon, her black bell of hair hanging forward, bent over a desk, writing, her right hand moving quickly, her left now and then impatiently tucking her hair behind one ear or the other. At length, she sat back and massaged her neck, emitting a long, satisfied sigh.

Marc stepped forward and brushed her hands aside, rubbing her stiff muscles for her.

She tilted her head back and looked up at him. "Did I wake you?"

He kissed her upside down. "No. I woke up because you were gone, but I didn't hear you until I was halfway down the stairs." He spun her chair around so she faced him, and crouched before her. "It's very beautiful music, Sharon."

She smiled. "I think so, too, but it still needs a lot of work."

There was a glow about her that made her even more achingly beautiful than ever before. It came from somewhere deep inside, and he wanted to capture it for all time, but knew there was no way he could, in spite of what he'd said so impulsively about wanting a long-term contract. He had to be realistic. All he could do was hope that he might be permitted to stay nearby for a time and see it whenever it was present.

"And do you know what makes it even more

beautiful—to me, anyway?" she said, then without waiting for an answer, rushed on. "It's because I did it for me! I realized tonight that of course I could still compose. I don't have to do it for the public. I don't have to do it for Ellis. I don't have to do it for anybody but myself and those I love. Only I was too unhappy for too long to realize that. I just told myself that I was doing nothing more for Ellis to steal, but if he doesn't know I'm doing it, there's no way he can steal it!"

Dropping from the chair, she knelt before him and flung her arms around his neck. "You gave me this, Marc! You showed me how to be happy again. And with my heart singing so loud inside me, I had to let it come out."

He squeezed his eyes tightly against the burning behind his lids, and held her in a bear hug, then stood with her still in his arms.

"Are you ready to go back to bed?"

She nestled close. "If that means what I think it means, then yes, I'm ready."

He lay beside her, smoothing her hair back, looking into her deep, dark eyes. He wished he could spend the rest of his life doing just that. "Did you mean it?" he asked.

"Mean what?"

He swallowed. "You said that you love me. I know it might just have been what some people say in the heat of the moment, but I want to know if it's true."

She ran her fingers into the curly hair of his beard. "I love you," she said, meeting his gaze without fear, giving him all the trust in her heart. "I'm sorry I didn't say it before I said it in . . .

passion, but I've never found it easy to say those words. I . . ." She bit her lip and looked away.

"Tell me," he said, turning her face back toward his. "Don't hide from me, Sharon."

There was shame in her eyes when she said, "He used to laugh at me for saying it. He said it was a 'puerile' thing to say. That was one of his favorite words for me, 'puerile.' So I guess I quit saying it unless it was sort of . . . dragged out of me."

"I don't suppose I'll ever hear any three words from you that mean more to me," he said huskily.

She smiled and said them again, then curled up, nestling against him with a sigh.

Marc turned out the light and lay there beside her, one hand on her hip, a dreadful melancholy stealing over him. What had he done? And far more important than what he had done, *what was he going to do?*

He wanted more than he'd believed he'd ever want anything again, to marry this woman in whose bed he lay. He wanted her children to be his. He wanted to have a child with her. He loved her. She loved him. What would be more logical than using that love to mesh their lives forever? Yet, when he should have asked her to be his wife, he had not. And he could not ask her without telling her his story. And if he did that, she would never, never marry him. If, through some great, good fortune, she did agree to be his wife, he knew he'd have to watch her trust in him erode.

So, he asked himself, how could he ever stay and marry her? He'd never forget her terror that day he'd been angry with her for refusing to break her date with the banker. He'd been able to make it better then, but over time, her fear of him would grow. He couldn't live with that, with knowing there was doubt in her heart. If only he hadn't told her he loved her before he knew what had been done to her. If only he hadn't made love to her without knowing how that bastard had undermined her self-confidence—not only as a musician, but as a woman. But he knew, too, that if he left her now, he could destroy her newly regained self-assurance before it reached its full bloom.

Restlessly, he shifted in the bed, his hands behind his head, sleep driven from his exhausted mind by more questions than there would ever be answers for. Beside him, Sharon turned her back, snuggled her rump against his thigh, and he shifted to rest one hand on the indentation of her waist. She was so perfect, this love of his, and tonight, she had started to compose again. In restoring her confidence in herself as a woman, he had given her the strength to branch out into other aspects of her life she'd believed were closed alleys. If he left her now, would she go right back to the way she'd been, hiding, not believing in herself, not creating anything, not trusting? There had to be a way! Maybe he'd be able to give her a parting gift that would make up for everything else. He would stay until he'd done that for her, at least.

Finally, he drew her deep into his arms and let her warmth seep through the icy cold of his spirit, as he drifted into a less than healing sleep.

She woke him when it was still dark, leaning over him, shaking him. "Marc!" There was the same kind of elation in her tone as there had been earlier, after she'd played her harp.

Sleepily, he drew her down against him, breathing in the perfume of her skin and hair. He snuggled her close, but she pulled back from him and reached out to turn on a light. He flung an arm over his eyes and groaned.

"Wake up," she said, getting up onto her knees and wrapping her hands around his wrist, trying to pull it down. "Let's go up to the mountain and surprise the McKenzies and the kids. I feel like skiing today. I feel like flying today!" He took his arm down and hauled himself to a sitting position. Her jubilation showed not only in her voice but in the shine of her eyes, the glow of her skin, and he could refuse her nothing.

"Get off this bed this minute," he warned her, his voice a deep growl, his eyes filled with love and laughter, "or we'll go flying all right, but not down a ski slope."

She paused to consider the alternative, then grinned, and he was delighted anew at this cheeky gamine he had discovered within her. "Well, we could always surprise them at lunchtime rather than breakfast," she said.

"Not," he said with a growl, "if you expect me to have any energy left for skiing."

Reluctantly, she backed off the bed and went to shower. This time, he had the good sense to let her do it by herself, and used the kids' bathroom for his own morning ablutions.

"I guess we should turn in," Marc said, casting a longing glance at Sharon. She was curled by the fire, half asleep, watching the lazy flames as they died down. The children and their hosts had long since gone to bed, replete after a New Year's dinner of slow-baked glazed ham and all the trimmings.

She and Marc had arrived in time for brunch to find the kids brown and happy and full of the things they'd done, the tumbles they'd taken, and the new skills they'd mastered. Harry and Zinnie, far from looking worn and exhausted as Sharon had feared they would, seemed even younger and more full of zest than before. It had been a perfect day for skiing. The sun shone brilliantly, and before she had skied two runs, Sharon's face was glowing with the beginnings of a burn, which, she assured Marc, would be a nice, brown tan by morning.

But now the day was over and a decision had to be made. Sharon knew it. Marc knew it. And they both knew that it was hers to make.

She turned and looked at him. She saw the question in his eyes, the longing, and felt such a surge of love and need, she didn't know how she could contain it. With a lithe movement, she got to her feet and came to stand before him. She looked miserable. The glow of the night before was gone. Her infectious exuberance of the day had died somewhere between Zinnie showing them the room that she'd assumed they'd share, and this moment.

"I'll take the couch in the den," she said quietly. "You have the bedroom." Bending, she kissed him and then stood erect. Careful not to touch her, he got to his feet as well.

"What's going to happen when we're home again, Sharon? Is it going to be like this, not only separate beds in separate rooms, but separate houses as well?"

Lifting her eyes to his, she said, "We'll work

something out, Marc. We'll find ways to be together."

"Be together?"

She turned pinker than her sunburn and looked down until he tilted her face up, one hand under her chin. "Sleep together," she said. "You could come over . . . after . . . after the kids are asleep, I guess."

"And leave before they get up." His tone was flat.

She slipped free of his hand. "Yes." It was a bare whisper of sound.

"I want more than that. I want us to be together all the time," he said, "not just sometimes. I want to go to sleep with you in my arms and wake up that way in the morning."

Her brows drew together. "*Live* with me?" Her voice cracked. "With us?"

After a moment, he nodded. "Yes. Sharon, we've come too far in our relationship for any other kind of arrangement."

She stared at him. *Except one,* she wanted to say, but could not. Because, when it came right down to it, even though they'd known each other to talk to for several months, even though she'd been aware of him on every level of her being since the first day she'd seen him, it was only a little more than a week since those incredible kisses they'd shared on Christmas Eve. Everything else that had happened to them since then, making love, declaring their love, sleeping together the whole time the kids were away, had been crammed into such a short space that neither of them could honestly say what they were ready for. And clearly, he was not ready to talk of anything but living together.

She shook her head. "I know that it's done all

the time now, Marc, and nobody thinks anything of it. I know lots of kids see their mothers living that way, but I just . . . can't. I'm sorry."

He could ask her to marry him. He knew that. He saw her dark, seeking eyes silently wondering why he did not. And he wanted to do it so bad, he hurt deep inside. But he knew that he couldn't. Because he was going to have to leave. Sometime. Sometime before it was too late, he was going to have to find a way to ease himself out of her life before he did even more damage to her than had already been done. So he didn't say it, and after a moment, she turned and went into the den.

Sharon was glad when the kids were back in school, when she could get back into the old, familiar routine of work and home and driving Jason to hockey and Scouts, Roxanne to figure skating and Brownies. They were activities that, if they did by some miracle manage to occur at the same time, were never in the same place. She felt like a juggler trying to keep a hundred balls in the air and was glad because it left her little time to think, little time to brood on the fact that the day after they arrived back from Mount Washington, Marc, with a brief word of good-bye, the key to his house so she could feed the stray cat he'd semiadopted, and a swift, hard kiss, had left on business.

She hadn't seen him or heard from him for nearly two weeks, when she looked out the kitchen window one morning and saw the camper parked in its familiar place on the other side of her patio wall. Her heart slammed hard against the inside of her ribs, making her knees feel like jelly and her eyes sting with tears.

She had to restrain herself not to run over there, and only the fact that the school bus was due in twenty minutes and she had to be at the library by ten-thirty prevented her giving in to the impulse. She stood there, gripping the edge of the sink, wondering when she would see him. Would he come to the library? Would he wait until that night? Would he come before the kids went to bed or after? Her body ached with needs he had aroused in her and then left unfilled for too long, needs that only he could take care of.

She had to hold herself very still when she saw him come loping down the front steps of his house, across the moist lawn, leaving silvery tracks in the grass, and leap up over the low wall at the edge of her patio. She met him at the back door, forgetting all the things she had planned to say to him, forgetting that she had decided to hold herself aloof until she knew where she stood with him. When he opened his arms she walked right into them, burrowing against his broad, warm, chest, moaning with relief at the knowledge that he was there again, holding her as if he'd never let her go.

"I missed you," he said, his voice a low rumble in his chest. "Where are the kids?"

"Upstairs getting dressed."

"Good, because I need to kiss you more than I've ever needed anything—food or drink or air or—" Or what, she never found out, because he stopped talking and started kissing, and she dimly head the door click shut, realizing that they were on the outside of it, wrapped in a blanket of rapidly growing body heat.

"Mom? Mom? Mommy!" The high-pitched wail finally got through to her, and Sharon shook her head, fighting off the sensual lethargy Marc's kisses had created. "Where are you?" Roxy called, beginnings of panic evident in her shrill voice.

"I have to go in," she said with a gasp, then called out, "Out here. I'll be right in! Marc, let me go. You shouldn't have come over at this time of day."

"Yes. I know. But I saw you in the window. I couldn't wait another minute to hold you." His golden eyes glittered between his half-closed lids, and she wanted to crawl back into his arms and never leave, but Roxy called again.

Sharon opened the door and stepped inside, just barely aware that Marc had not followed her in, that he was the one who had closed the door behind her.

"What were you doing out there?" Both kids gaped at her. "You don't have any shoes on, Mom." Jason scowled. He wasn't allowed outside barefoot in January!

"I just went out for minute to see if . . . if the snowdrops were blooming. I thought I saw something white in the planter."

Jason shrugged with utter lack of interest in flowers, and Roxy handed her a hairbrush. "Can you fix my hair, Mommy?" With shaking hands, she did as her daughter asked, then made sure both children had their lunches before sending them out to wait for the bus.

She heard Jason's whoop of delight. "Hey, look! Marc's home!" and echoed it in her heart even though she knew that this was not Marc's home and probably never would be. She was suddenly frightened as much for Jason as she was for herself. He would be crushed when his hero left. Was Marc aware of that? Was that why he'd avoided coming in while the kids were getting ready for school? It didn't make sense, she thought, sitting down at the kitchen table with her second cup of coffee. He was the one who had wanted them to live together, wasn't he? Had he thought maybe the kids wouldn't notice? Or was it simply that he had changed his mind?

She dropped her head into her hands, her fingers shoved through her hair, and never even heard the door open. She wasn't aware that Marc was in the room until he lifted her out of her chair and held her high against his chest, nuzzling the front of her robe open with his chin and nose.

She struggled, and he set her on her feet but didn't let her go. "Marc," she said earnestly, "we need to talk."

"Sharon," he said just as earnestly, "we need to make love." He kissed her long and hard, until all the arguments she might ever have considered were gone like smoke in the wind. "Here?" he said with a grin she couldn't resist, "or"—with a toss of his head—"up there?"

"I only get to pick one?"

He laughed and scooped her up again, heading for the stairs. "For starters, love. Just for starters."

For the first time in three years, Sharon phoned in sick when she wasn't.

Nine

"Marc, do you read music?" Sharon looked up from her desk, half turning to face him. He glanced up from the book he was reading and nodded.

"Would you . . ." Her voice cracked and, with a sheaf of papers trembling visibly in her hand, she got to her feet, gnawing on her lower lip. Marc stood, caught her in agitated mid-stride, and held her still. She drew in a deep breath and started again. "Would you like to try this with me?" She put the papers into his hand and turned her back quickly as if she couldn't bear to watch his face while he looked at them.

" 'For Harmonica and Harp' . . . Sharon, yes! Yes, of course I want to try this with you! Sweetheart, it'll be great!" Spinning her around, he gave her a quick kiss and then he was striding out of the house. "I'll be right back," he said before he closed the door.

She heard his feet thud as he jumped back over the wall on his return trip, and when the door opened again, she was seated on her stool, fingers caressing her harp strings, waiting for him.

With his music sheets on a stand before him, he sat nearby and listened to the light, airy intro she had written, then came in with his part. At once, she stopped him. "No. Not like that. Ease in. You can't overwhelm the harp at this point. So come in softly, like a hint of a breeze slipping through the branches of a tree to find the wind chimes hanging there."

He grinned at her. "What are you, a musician or a poet?" But he tried it again, and she smiled encouragement as he let his breathy music slip up unobtrusively and blend with hers, until the combined tones sounded the way she had intended. Slowly, she led him through the work, his harmonica growing stronger, rustling the leaves, making branches sway, dying down again and leaving the chimes to fade away into stillness.

More than an hour had passed before she pronounced that part of the composition just right. Over and over, she had taken back his score and rewritten it, just as she had her own. Rubbing his back, he arched and stretched. "You're a perfectionist. It sounded just great to me the way it was before those last changes. How did you know it would sound better the new way?"

"I just knew. Do you want to quit? Is your back tired? How about your lips?"

He leaned over and kissed her. "I don't know. How about my lips?"

She laughed, and it was a joyous sound. "Your lips seem to be holding up all right."

"Then let's keep going." He'd sit there till he rotted if it would keep that wonderful glow of hers alive.

They were well into the second section of her

new work when Sharon suddenly realized that they had an audience of two. Her hands fell from the strings, and she stood, knocking her stool onto its side, crowding out past Marc, and flinging herself into her sister's arms.

"Jeanie, Max! What are you doing here?"

"Oh, I missed you, Sharon!" Jeanie hugged her tightly, then shoved her away, her eyes full of questions. "You were playing! I can't believe it! And it was so beautiful! It's new, isn't it? It's yours!"

"Yes," Sharon said softly. "Mine, Jeanie. All mine."

"It's wonderful to see you playing again, to hear it." Jeanie wiped two tears from her tanned cheeks, and then hugged her again.

Sharon stood back and looked up at her tall little sister. "It's wonderful to see you two as well, but aren't you a couple of weeks short of a full honeymoon?" They'd meant to stay away until the middle of February, and it was only the second.

Max beamed so wide, his lean face threatened to split, and Jeanie gave a little shrug. "We . . . well, we just wanted to come home. We missed you." She moved away from her sister. "Hello, Marc. It's nice to see you again. I didn't know you were such a good musician."

Marc stepped forward and accepted Max's firm handshake and Jeanie's quick kiss on the cheek. "The fact is, I'm not such a good musician. I always thought I was more adequate, in an amateur sort of way, of course. But tonight I've learned that I'm not only amateur, I'm slow and a little bit stupid and don't know a B-sharp from an A-flat. And if I did, I wouldn't be able to get them in at the right time and place and with the proper cadence."

"Marc!" Sharon stared at him. "Have I been that hard on you?"

His smile was slow and filled with love he made no attempt to hide. "No, of course not. But I love to tease you because it makes your eyes glitter. Seriously, though," he added, turning to Jeanie again, "I have learned an awful lot from your sister tonight."

Sharon met Jeanie's eyes and read a hundred questions in them. Quickly, she turned away, terribly aware of the bright burning color in her cheeks. Somehow, Jeanie finding Marc in her house at nine-thirty in the evening was even worse than Zinnie and Harry finding him in the chalet at breakfast time.

"Well, let's not just stand here," she said quickly. "Come on in and sit down. Are you hungry? Did you drive from Victoria? Do you need dinner or a snack or what? And where are your bags? I'll go and make a pot of coffee unless you'd rather have drinks?"

Max laughed at his sister-in-law's jerky movements and staccato speech. "Hey, relax, Sharon. We're family, aren't we?" He slung an arm around her shoulder and bumped her up against his side, much as his brother Rolph had a habit of doing. "I'll get the bags. Jeanie can help you make coffee—decaf, please, for my wife, and she will need a snack, but I'm not hungry."

"I'll give you a hand with the bags," Marc said, "and then I'll get on home. See you tomorrow, Sharon?"

Standing half in the dining room, half in the living room on her way to the kitchen, she looked at him with longing mingled with understanding. He was going to absent himself in order not to cause her any further embarrassment—or maybe to save himself some. But if she let him go, it was as if she were saying that he was nothing more than a neighbor who had come in to share a musical evening with her. She didn't want to deny him to her family.

"Don't you want coffee?" she asked in a small voice.

With a smile, he shook his head, mouthed the word "tomorrow," and went out to help Max.

"He's even more gorgeous than I remembered," said Jeanie, dropping bread into the toaster. "But I must say I was surprised to see him here with you. The last I heard, you couldn't stand him."

"Uh, well, he's not as bad as I thought."

Jeanie nodded. "So it seems. You see a lot of him?"

"Uh . . . yes. Quite a bit."

Jeanie reached into an upper cabinet where Sharon kept the spices and brought down a bottle of cinnamon. She gave her sister a quizzical look. "Dare I ask if this is serious? And if it is, why did the guy take off like that?"

Sharon shrugged. "Just being polite, I guess. He knew we'd want to talk."

"We can't talk in front of him?"

"Well, you know. Family." She shrugged again.

"Jase must be in seventh heaven if you've made friends with his hero." The toast popped, and Jeanie put it on a plate and began slathering it with butter, then added sugar and cinnamon. When Sharon didn't answer, she glanced at her over her shoulder, dropped the knife, and ignored it when it fell to the floor with a clatter.

"Sharon! What's the matter?" Gently, she led her sister to a chair and sat her down. She grabbed a fistful of tissues from a box on the counter and stuffed them into Sharon's hand. "Hey, come on. Tell me what's wrong."

"He's more than Jason's hero, and I've done more than make friends with him. I'm in love with him. And he says he loves me."

Jeanie plopped onto a chair and looked hard at Sharon's woeful face. "This," she said, "is reason for tears?"

"It is when we have to sneak around together. We hire a sitter, say we're going out, and sometimes do, but then go back to his place and, well, you know. Or we wait until the kids are in bed and he comes here, but then I make him leave before morning. It's a lousy way to live, Jeanie, and I hate it more and more every day. But there just doesn't seem to be any other way." She wiped her eyes and blew her nose, then sat up straight.

Jeanie remembered her toast, got up, and brought it back to the table. The aroma of coffee began to fill the room. "There's a marvelous institution called marriage," she said. "I recommend it highly."

"I'm glad to hear that," Max said, coming in and taking her by the wrist, bringing her hand and her toast up to his mouth. He grabbed a huge bite, just missing her fingers, which she folded into a fist to wave threateningly.

"You said you weren't hungry! Go make your own toast, McKenzie."

He ruffled her already messy hair until it stood out around her head like a glowing bush. "This," he said to Sharon as soon as he'd swallowed, "is what I have to put up with. Orders, orders, day and night. I have to do this, I have to do that. And she doesn't have to do one solitary thing. She won't clean up after me, she won't cook my meals, she won't iron my shirts, she won't wash my car. She won't—"

"Hang around to listen to this garbage," said Jeanie, standing up. Quickly, Max took her chair and swung her down onto his lap, where she stayed with every indication of willingness, one arm linked around his shoulder, feeding him bites of her last slice of toast.

"And what was Auntie Sharon's reaction to our news?" Max asked.

Sharon stared. "Did you say 'Auntie'?"

Jeanie's grin was as wide as her husband's. "I hadn't told her yet. I was waiting for you to come back. But that's why we came home, Sharon. Being morning sick in a hotel isn't the nicest thing in the world."

Sharon hugged them both. "The way I remember it, morning sickness isn't the nicest thing in the world no matter where you are, but . . ." She shook her head in delight and disbelief. "I thought you were planning to wait a year."

Max shrugged and laughed. "So did we. But we forgot to take into account the fact that while our cave had water, some food, a sleeping bag, and a blanket, it lacked one rather important element— a drugstore."

"But we couldn't be happier," Jeanie said. "We're going to name him Dungeon."

"We are not," Max contradicted. "We are going to name her Caverna." Both laughed as if this had become a comfortable and beloved argument.

"But since we can't agree," Jeanie said, sliding off Max's lap and putting more bread in the toaster, "we'll likely end up calling him George."

"Martha."

Sharon poured coffee and a large glass of milk that her sister drank without protest.

* * *

"He doesn't want to marry me," Sharon said the next day when she and Jeanie were alone, the kids having reluctantly gone off to school, and Max was out for his morning run. Jeanie, looking slightly green, sat at the kitchen table nibbling crackers and sipping weak tea. "At least that's the only conclusion I've been able to come to, since he hasn't mentioned the word."

"You don't suppose he's already married to someone else, do you?"

Sharon frowned. Oddly enough, not once had that thought occurred to her. But it was certainly a possibility. "All he'd told me," she said, "is that he was married, and his wife and son died. I'm not sure how. He doesn't talk about it."

"But no suggestion that he's looking for any kind of permanent relationship with you?"

"He did ask if he could move in here with us, but I don't want that. If he's not ready to commit, if there's the chance that he's going to leave again come spring, it would be too difficult not only for me, but for the kids, when he goes." With a hint of uncharacteristic bitterness, she said, "He feeds a stray cat too. I've often wondered if he means to take her with him."

"Does he know about your marriage?"

Sharon nodded. "Everything about it." Things, she reflected, that not even Jeanie knew. She often wondered if that was part of his reason for not wanting to make a commitment to her. Was he afraid that she would go back to being the way she had been, and he'd be stuck with a frigid wife?

"But the fact that you're playing again, composing again, is due to him, isn't it?"

Sharon smiled slowly. "Yes. No matter what happens, I'll always have that to remember. It was the happiness, Jeanie. He made me so free inside, so full of joy that it just came spilling out. It's as if it's been pent up for so long that there's no end to it. The music is renewed inside me, and I have to write it down. I'm compelled to play it."

"Nothing could make me happier," Jeanie said, squeezing Sharon's hand. "What was that piece the two of you were doing together last night?"

"I wrote that for us. 'For Harmonica and Harp.' I know the two instruments aren't traditionally even considered to be in the same world, but it seemed right for us. And I think it worked, but maybe I was too close. How did it sound? How much did you hear?"

"Not much. Not enough." Jeanie smiled. "We couldn't believe what we were hearing—or I couldn't. Max thought there was something wrong when I came to a dead halt on the front porch and nearly dug my fingers into the bones of his wrist. He started to talk, and I just reached up and put my hand over his mouth and told him to listen, for God's sake, just listen, that he was hearing a miracle! But then a little gust of wind came up, and he said miracle or no miracle, I was not standing out there to get chilled."

Her eyes shone with a silver glow as she looked at Sharon. "I was so happy to hear that music coming from your harp!" She clutched her sister's hands in her own. "Don't ever let anything stop you again. Promise me. Sell it under a pseudonym if you must, but keep doing it!"

"I promise," Sharon said, and explained that she was doing it for herself, that it wasn't for sale under any name, just in case Ellis found out and managed to steal it.

"But that means the public won't have it," said Jeanie sadly.

"It doesn't matter. I have it. We have it." Then, getting to her feet, she glanced at the clock. "But since my livelihood comes from my job at the library, I'd better not be late."

"Hi." The deep voice just behind her sent Sharon spinning around, nearly crashing into the cart of books she was shelving. "Got time for lunch today?"

"You bet!" Her face shone with love and gladness, and he wished there was time to go home for lunch. What he wanted for lunch demanded privacy. Instead, when the head librarian came back from her own break, they made do with a corner booth near the back of the little cafe near the library.

Crowding in next to her, he slid an arm around her waist and drew her tightly against his side. "Can I kiss you here?"

Leaning her head back against his shoulder, she said, "You can kiss me anywhere."

When he came up for air, he murmured, "And how about 'everywhere'?"

She swallowed and inched away from him before she was tempted to disgrace herself in front of the young waitress who was approaching. "That," she whispered, "comes later."

When they were alone again, she said, "You didn't have to take off like that last night, Marc. You'd have been welcome to stay."

He gave that little half-shrug she found so charming, and quirked a crooked smile at her. "I didn't want to intrude, and I didn't know what you intended to tell your sister about us."

She looked him square in the eye. "I told her," she said, "that we're in love and sleeping together—when we can do it discreetly."

He looked away from her, stirred his coffee, and then turned the spoon over and over in his fingers, like a baton twirler. Glancing up, his eyes shadowed by drawn brows, he said, "And she asked why we aren't getting married."

Sharon nodded slowly. "More or less."

"What did you tell her?"

This time, she shrugged and looked down at the table. "There wasn't much I could tell her, was there? Except that . . ." She shrugged again.

"Except that you haven't been asked."

Still keeping her eyes downcast, she said quietly, "That's right."

"How is she with a shotgun?"

Sharon tilted her head back and gave him a long, hard look. "Jeanie is my sister," she said, "not my father. And I'm not pregnant or in any danger of getting that way, so I don't think talk of shotguns is appropriate. Besides, I am thirty-seven years old. I make my own decisions about my life."

When the waitress had served her chicken strips and his cheeseburger, he nibbled on a fry. "If that were a decision you were being asked to make, what do you think it would be?"

"That's an unfair question, Marc."

His shoulders slumped. "Yes. I guess it is."

He slid out of her side of the small booth and over to the other side, and ate his lunch in thoughtful silence.

Then, locking his hand around her slender wrist, he leaned forward and said hoarsely, "If it were my decision to make, mine alone, then we'd be married right now. But it's not, Sharon. I . . .

oh, hell, this isn't the time or the place, and there are things you need to know about me. Can you come over tonight? Right after work?"

She looked at him, searching his pain-filled eyes. "Just tell me one thing, Marc. You said that your wife had died. Is that the truth?"

"Yes," he said.

"Do you have another wife somewhere else?"

His eyes widened in shock. "No! No, Sharon. I swear it. I have loved two women in my life. You are the second one. I never even thought about marrying again until I met you."

"Then I'll come over tonight. Max and Jeanie are taking the kids out for dinner and to a movie anyway, since it's Friday. I was going to go, too, but I'll just call and say I've made other plans."

"Okay." He nodded once, got to his feet, and stood looking down at her. "Just remember, Sharon. I love you."

"I'll remember," she said, but doubted if he heard her. He had spun around and was gone.

You can't do this, he told himself, pacing back and forth across his small living room.

You have to do it, another part of him argued.

Do it, and you lose her.

Don't and you lose her.

So, you lose either way, but wouldn't it be better for her to remember you with some respect, for her to think of you as a man who was simply unable to make a decision, than a . . . Marc pounded his fist into the palm of his hand and continued pacing, knowing that no matter what he did, it could be exactly the wrong thing. *She loves me. She'll believe in me.*

He hated his own cowardice, telling himself

that there were no guarantees in life and this whole situation had gone on too long. He was in no better shape than he'd been six years ago, a reeling drunk in the back alleys of Toronto.

Then, his father had found him, dragged him out of there, pasted the broken pieces back together, and sent him out to find a soul to put inside the shell he'd become. He had found that soul, but it hadn't been enough, not until Sharon had filled the emptiness and given the body and soul what they lacked—a heart. What kind of a man was he if he refused to tell her the truth because it was a risk?

Wheeling around, taking the stairs two at a time, he chose a positive action over the negative ones he'd been taking. He had time to shower before Sharon got here. He didn't want her to have to smell his gutless fear on him.

Sharon knocked. There was no reply, although the lights were on and the drapes wide open. She knocked again then opened the door. From upstairs, there came the rushing sound of the shower, and she wandered around the living room, too nervous to sit. What could he have to tell her that was so terrible? When he'd left the cafe, his face had been so pale, she'd wondered whether he was safe behind the wheel. Her relief at seeing his camper parked where it belonged had gone to her head, making her dizzy, telling her exactly how much of her worry she had stuffed down where it wouldn't be visible even to her. That was something she had learned to do a long time ago. Recently, though, she'd been unlearning it. With Marc's help, and in the warmth of his loving care, she had been unlearning a good many lessons from the past.

Her biggest fear now was that the future might be in jeopardy. *What future?* a little voice asked her. *Have you ever been given any reason to hope for a future with Marc?* She knew that even if she hadn't, until today, she'd harbored a hope, a crazy, unquenchable hope that this relationship was the ultimate one.

Her restless feet carried her into the little den Marc used as an office, and she turned the picture frame on his desk, finding a snapshot of herself that she hadn't known about. When had he taken it? In the summer or fall, obviously, since she was wearing a sleeveless blouse and the tree behind her was in full leaf. A breeze had caught her hair, lifting it back from her face, and she was laughing at something, likely one of the kids. Six weeks ago, she'd have been horrified to know that her next-door neighbor was taking telephoto pictures of her. Now, she smiled and set it back down again, loving him just a little bit more.

At that moment, his fax machine came to life, startling her. She spun around and looked at it as the paper came flopping out into the basket.

The fax was addressed to Jean-Marc St.-Clair, with a string of degrees after the name, and came from a law office somewhere in Toronto. The name Jean-Marc St.-Clair rang a distant bell, and she frowned. It was an unpleasant bell, and while she realized that the fax was not meant for her, she saw at once it was, however, *about* her! She read on:

Ref. your client, Sharon Leslie:
  There is no record of Sharon Leslie ever

having signed a power of attorney to Ellis Murcady or any other individual or organization. Therefore, we feel that his having copyrighted her material in his own name during the term of their marriage constitutes a fraud. After consultation with certain members of the music community, particularly staff at the Royal Conservatory where Ms. Leslie was trained, we further feel that a strong case can be made to show that past, and very possibly present, work credited to the current Mrs. Murcady is uniquely that of Ms. Leslie.

In private consultations, several justices—including your esteemed father—have given their opinion that Ms. Leslie would have just cause to bring suit against her former spouse and have every expectation of winning such a suit, regaining the royalties lost to her. Naturally, whatever she might compose at this time can certainly be copyright by her with no fear of Mr. Murcady's being able to claim the work or any proceeds from it.

It ended with kind, personal regards and a scrawled set of initials.

Sharon stared at the paper for several seconds, dimly aware that the shower had shut off upstairs. Could this be true? Could she win back what Ellis had stolen? And even if that weren't possible, was her name really her own, her present work her personal property? She picked the paper up and gazed at it again. That was what it said. She couldn't be misinterpreting it, could she? Still holding it, she turned to go upstairs to Marc. He would know! He was a lawyer and—

She came to an abrupt halt as the knowledge slammed into her. *He was the lawyer who had requested this information. He was, of course, Jean-Marc St.-Clair.* As she gazed at the name the distant unease was replaced by a flood of memory. Mentally, she deleted his beard, shortened his hair, deducted several inches of muscular shoulder development gained over six years of manual labor, and she had it.

My God! Jean-Marc St.-Clair was a man who had been accused of murdering his own wife and child, then was let go for lack of evidence!

She clenched her fingers on the fax, staring at the name, feeling again the horror she had felt at the time, remembering how bitterly aware she had been of the notorious case of the fine, upstanding crown prosecutor accused of such a heinous crime, the swirling controversy, the innuendo, the shock and disgust when he was set free. It had meant more to her than to most people because of the precarious position she was in herself. Why hadn't she recognized him? Now that she knew, she could see him as he'd looked six years ago, clean-shaven, neatly dressed, face drawn with weariness or grief—or possibly fear. She had followed the story as it unfolded, watching it on the news, reading it in the daily papers, and then, suddenly, it was all over.

Case dismissed at the preliminary hearing because of lack of evidence.

She had, she told herself, not expected anything different. Men could beat their wives and get away with it. It happened every day. That she knew all too well.

She wasn't the only one horrified by that abrupt

summation of the case. The rumors began to run rampant; there were editorials that hinted slyly and suggested artfully that justice had not been done.

The accused was an officer of the court. His father, two brothers, and one sister carried on the tradition of the old, prestigious family law firm, of which he had been a member before accepting the position of crown prosecutor. His grandfather was a retired supreme court justice. One of his uncles was a senator. The St.-Clair family was solid establishment, wealthy and well-known. Was it any wonder, asked people on the streets, that he had been released for "lack of evidence"? Evidence against a man such as Jean-Marc St.-Clair could easily be suppressed. An ordinary man would have gotten life. A wealthy St.-Clair got off.

And this, she knew, as sickness rose up to choke her, was what Marc was going to tell her about.

"No," she whispered, unaware that she had crumpled the paper in her hands. "No, I don't want to hear it. I don't want to know!" As she grabbed up the coat she had left on the brass hall stand, the ball of paper fell to the floor. Without seeing it, without seeing anything, she let herself out of his house, closing the door as quietly as she had opened it.

If he was innocent, why didn't he tell her long ago? she wondered. If he was innocent, why did he run as he clearly had? Why hadn't he stayed and fought the innuendo? Instead, he'd become a wanderer, drifting around the world, afraid to go home again, afraid to face up to his accusers because . . . Because in spite of the findings of the court, the rumors were true? If he hadn't done it, who had? No other killer had ever been found!

Sharon reached into her coat pocket and grabbed her keys, tore open her car door, and flung herself behind the wheel, jamming the ignition key in and starting the engine. She backed out of his drive recklessly, swung onto the street, and laid rubber half the way down the block of her nice, quiet residential neighborhood.

Marc jerked open the door and stared after her, wondering what in the hell was going on. Then he stooped and picked up the crumpled piece of paper from the floor.

He smoothed it out, read it, and sat down hard in a chair. Burying his face in his hands, he groaned. "Sharon, oh, Sharon," he whispered after a few minutes, tilting his head back and staring blindly at the ceiling. "Why couldn't you have believed in me, love? Why did you have to be like everyone else? We aren't strangers! You know me! Why couldn't you wait and hear what I had to say?"

But he knew the answer to that. He'd known it all along: Sharon had no reason to trust and every reason not to. Wearily, he got to his feet and went upstairs.

It was time, he knew, to move on.

"What am I doing?" Sharon asked herself just under an hour later. She was miles away from home, far up the highway, heading north and still going. She slowed, pulled over to the side, and leaned her head against the wheel. "I ran. I panicked and I ran." Presently, she drove on again, found a place to turn around, and headed back. What had she done with the fax she'd read? She frowned, trying to remember, but all she could recall were the words, the name that suddenly triggered a memory, those dreadful feelings of fear and betrayal. She thought she'd probably put it back in the basket where it had appeared. She must have. So Marc wouldn't know she'd been there. He wouldn't know she'd read it, realized who he was, and fled because of that.

She felt sick again, but this time because she had let the past overshadow the present. She knew Marc. She loved him and trusted him implicitly. He was not Ellis. He did not hit women and children. He had not killed his wife and son. The lack of evidence against him surely proved that. The fact that no one else had ever been charged meant simply that no suspect had ever been found. It had likely been one of those weird, random killings with no motive other than thrill-seeking. She remembered that there had been some talk of devil-worship cults, or secret initiations, all nebulous, all completely unprovable—just as the charges against Marc had been.

A glance at her dashboard clock showed her it was long past the time when he'd been expecting her. She'd got off work early, but not that early. What must he be thinking? He'd be frantic, wondering where she was. By now he'd have called the police, all the hospitals, likely gone out and searched himself. She glanced at her speedometer and took her foot off the gas. Getting ticketed for speeding would only slow her down. Should she stop and phone him? Yes. Of course!

Pulling into the next service station, she listened to his phone ring and ring and ring. He wasn't home. Poor Marc. He was out looking for her, as anxious as she would be if he had failed to show up for an important appointment at the right time. What was she going to tell him to excuse her lateness? She sighed. The truth, of course. He deserved that from her. It wasn't going to be easy, but she'd have to do it.

It seemed to take forever to get home, and when she did, his truck wasn't there. She went to his house to see if he'd left a message, but the door was locked.

On her own back door she found what she'd been looking for, and tore the sealed envelope open eagerly, wondering why he'd bothered to seal it. Leaning against the door, she stared at the words, turning the paper so the porch light shone on the page, trying to make sense of some very plain words, words that kept blurring before her eyes. No. No. She was reading it all wrong. That wasn't what it said. *It wasn't! It wasn't! It wasn't!*

Ten

Only . . . time proved that it was. Marc was gone. It wouldn't have taken him long to pack. As befitted a drifter, a man ready to wander away at moment's notice, he'd had very little that wouldn't fit into his camper.

The next week, a For Sale sign appeared on the lawn next door, and by that time the cat, which he had never named, had made the transition to being fed at Sharon's house, sleeping curled in a small box just inside the basement window.

"You have to do something, Sharon." Jeanie, who was visiting with Max for the weekend, paced around the living room. She stopped at the side of her sister's shrouded harp and glared at it. It hadn't been uncovered in weeks.

"I know," Sharon said evenly. "I've been doing it. I'm . . . getting over him. It's not going to be easy, and it won't happen overnight, but there's nothing else I can do that I haven't done already. Ads in every daily paper in every major city in North America haven't brought a response. I've been in touch with the law office in Toronto that sent the fax. They either don't know where he is, or won't tell me. It's been over a month. If he wanted to get in touch, he would. He knows where I am, Jeanie."

Jeanie knelt before her sister, looking intently into the dark, sorrowful eyes. "Once, not so very long ago," she said slowly, "you sent me after the man I love. I went, scared stiff-and-spitless that he might send me away. But I had to do it. I took your word for it that it was worth the chance. Why don't you do the same, Sharon?"

"I would! Oh, Jeanie, believe me, I would if I knew where to start looking! But don't forget, this is a big world, and he could be anywhere."

Jeanie sighed and nodded, then got to her feet and wandered into the kitchen to find something good to eat, something incredibly sweet and sticky and calorie-rich. Lord, she was going to look like a whale before her baby was born!

"Jeanie! Max! Wake up!" The knocking on their door brought both of them wide awake in an instant. Jumping up, Max dragged on a robe and threw one at Jeanie before he swung open the door, blinking in the light from the hallway.

"Sharon, what's wrong?"

"Nothing! Nothing! But . . . will you take the kids with you when you leave in the morning? It's spring break, and I've already talked to Zinnie. She said they can stay with her and Harry."

Jeanie said, "Sure, but . . . where are you going?"

"I'm going to Montreal."

Jeanie breathed a sigh of relief. "Marc! You've heard from him." She laughed happily and said,

"When did he call? What did he say? Where has he been?"

"He didn't call. But I woke up knowing where he is!" She didn't tell her sister that Grandma Margaret had told her in a dream. She knew Max thought the whole thing about their Gypsy ancestress was a crock.

"What?" Max shook his head. "How could you—"

Jeanie interrupted, eyes full of light. "Never mind. She knows."

"Yes." Sharon's conviction shone in her face. "Where would you go if you were hurt, if you'd gone everywhere else in the world and not found peace?"

"Here, of course," her sister said with full understanding. "I wouldn't even try every other place in the world. I'd come home to you."

"That's what Marc has done. I'm sure of it. He's gone home. He must have. But even if he hasn't, his family will know where he is. I'm going to them. I'll make them tell me where he is, and then I'm going to bring him home!"

Behind her, Jason rubbed sleep out of his eyes and said, "Yeah! Go for it, Mom!"

Jeanie repeated the phrase as she hugged her sister. "Damn right! Go for it, Mom . . ."

Max gave a long-suffering sigh. "But there is absolutely nowhere you can go at three o'clock in the morning except to bed. Does anybody mind?"

Sharon laughed and shooed her son toward his room. "You guys go ahead. I have to pack a bag." Then, biting her lip, she looked at the others with consternation. "I wondered why Zinnie had such a hard time understanding me at first. I guess I woke her up. Oh, my goodness, I hope she'll forgive me!"

"What she wouldn't forgive," Max said, laughing, "is not being made a part of this expedition of yours. I'm sure she was thrilled to get a call in the middle of the night if it would further the course of true love. Now, good night, dear sister-in-law. Please. Good night!"

A filthy scum of used snow lay at the side of the street. Naked trees cast lacy shadows on the sidewalk, and floating clouds interspersed with blue patches of sky reflected in puddles where slush and ice had melted temporarily. Sharon stood and watched the taxi drive off, and then she was alone except for a mailman far down the long block, heading her way. She gazed at the tall, wrought-iron gates set into the gray stone walls surrounding the ancient, massive house.

It was a forbidding place, this St.-Clair family home, even though one side of the gates stood open and the drive was neatly plowed, even dry in spots, with wisps of steam arising, as if the fitful spring sun had been enough to warm it. She had no idea who actually lived there, if it was Marc's grandparents, or his parents, or perhaps all of them. She had thought about making an appointment with one of his brothers or his sister at the law offices, but this was a personal, not a business matter, and a personal approach was the right one. And surely whomever she found within that stone pile of a house would know where Marc was. The question, however, was would they tell her?

A uniformed maid answered the door, and Sharon blinked with surprise. Nobody she knew had a uniformed maid! This was going to be harder than she'd anticipated. In rusty French, she asked to speak to "Madame," hoping that was a logical request. What if no one lived there but Marc's grandfather?

To her relief, the maid stepped back and said, "This way, please. You are expected." Sharon thought she must have been mistaken. It was a long time since she'd spoken or heard French. Except, she thought with a stab of pain, the love words Marc had whispered to her in the endless nights they'd shared.

The maid took her coat and gloves, placed them in a huge armoire, and then led the way across an entry hall that was almost as big as Sharon's entire main floor. It had an elegant, sweeping staircase leading up to a gallery, and it was this way the maid took her. The stairs were marble with a deep red runner held in place with solid brass rods. As she followed the woman down a corridor leading off the gallery, Sharon felt as if she had entered a museum. Dark wainscoting seemed to eat up the light cast by bulbs recessed into an extraordinarily high ceiling. Suddenly, a sense of unreality came over her. She was completely out of her element. If this house was indicative of Marc's background, it pointed out only too sharply the differences between them. He was exotic South Pacific shells; she was sand dollars from the Lantzville beach. She didn't belong here any more than she'd have belonged at Buckingham Palace.

When the maid knocked briefly and swung open a set of nine-feet-tall double doors, the black-dressed woman actually curtsied, for heaven's sake! Then, stepping aside for Sharon to enter, she announced that the nurse was there and backed out, shutting the enormous doors, leaving Sharon on the inside.

On the far side of the room, an elderly, diminutive woman dressed in a red track suit sat erect on a hassock, toasting marshmallows on a very long fork over a blazing fire. Her hair was piled high in elaborate lavender curls and twists, and she peered with interest at Sharon.

A quick, infectious smile broke across her face as she bade her guest to come in and sit down, and offered her a marshmallow by holding out the fork with an already golden brown morsel on the end. The color of it reminded Sharon of Marc's eyes, and she had to blink to keep tears from forming in her own.

"Bon jour," she said, sitting on the edge of the chair the woman indicated and shaking her head at the offer of the marshmallow. The woman shrugged in a manner that was so familiar and so dear, Sharon was again forced to blink back tears. Quickly, she introduced herself and explained that she was there under false pretenses. She wasn't the expected nurse but a personal friend of Jean-Marc's, and she dearly hoped that someone could tell her where to find him.

"Ah . . ." said the elderly woman. "You are, perhaps, a lady-love of my grandson?" She had spoken in English, faintly accented.

"Yes, but not 'a' lady-love. I am the only one," she corrected Marc's grandmother gently.

Black-penciled eyebrows rose, one higher than the other. "So? You seem sure of this."

"Yes. I am sure of it."

"How is it, then, that you do not know where Jean-Marc is?"

"We had a misunderstanding."

The woman licked her fingers and placed another marshmallow on the fork. "A lovers' quarrel?" she asked gleefully, leaning forward to poke her marshmallow close to the coals, only taking her bright eyes off Sharon for an instant. "Lovers' quarrels are wonderful! Tell me all about yours."

It was a command that Sharon ignored. "Wonderful?" she asked. "What is so wonderful about them?"

"Why . . . making up, of course." Her eyes twinkled as she cocked her head to one side as if waiting for Sharon to say something, and when she did not, turned her attention once again to her cooking task.

"Enough for me," she said, eating the last marshmallow. "I shall order coffee now, and cakes."

"But . . . the nurse?"

"Pah! She can come tomorrow. Today, I wish to speak with you, to hear your story. Begin."

"Madame, please, I really must not waste time. Yours or mine. Can you tell me where Marc-er, Jean-Marc—is? I truly need to see him. To talk to him."

The woman nodded. "Ah, yes. But does my grandson want to see you?"

Sharon was unable to control the tears that flooded up in response to the question. "I don't know," she whispered. "I only know I have to try. Madame, please help me."

Leaning forward, the old woman patted her hands and said, "Of course I will. Only . . . first you must tell me all about it."

To her surprise, over coffee and cakes, it was easy for Sharon to explain in full detail not only the story of her time with Marc, but of her marriage and the insecurities she'd been left with. And when she was finished, Madame St.-Clair nodded slowly. "Yes. I can see how you might have been confused and frightened for just a small while and run away. It is a shame my grandson did not wait to speak with you. But that is his way. When he is 'urt, he goes to hide."

"Then you understand? Where is he hiding, Madame?"

"Where?" The question was accompanied by widening eyes, lifted brows, and hands spread palms-up in a helpless gesture. "Where? I do not know! How would I know? I'm just an old lady. No one tells me anything."

"Oh! But . . ." Sharon couldn't hide her dismay. "I see. Thank you." She got to her feet. "Forgive me for taking up your time, Madame."

"Oh, sit down, sit down, child. I did not say I couldn't find out where he is. I will ask his father. My son Reginald always knows where Jean-Marc is. They are close." She crossed her fingers. "Like this, no?" She reached for a large, black rotary-dial telephone.

Sharon sat on the edge of her chair watching the play of expression and emotion cross the old woman's face as she spoke in rapid French. Finally, with a sigh, and a moue of sadness, Madame hung up.

"My son . . . he says Jean-Marc does not want to see you, and that I am not to tell you where he is."

Again, Sharon stood. Holding her hand out, she said in a taut voice that just hovered on the edge of a wobble, "Thank you, Madame St.-Clair, for trying. Good-bye."

"What? No. You must not say good-bye, my dear child. Come, we will take a drive together, you and I. You tell me you have not been to my city for many years. I cannot let you go without showing you around." Again, she reached for the telephone, and this time Sharon understood that she was ordering her car brought around.

Argument was useless. Whatever she said was overridden and pooh-poohed. There was time, Madame assured her, for everything, and all would work out for the best. With a floor-length mink draped over her red track suit, and her feet stuffed into fleece-lined boots, Marc's grandmother hurried her guest out to the chauffeur-driven car. Sharon, she ordered, was not to worry but to enjoy.

Sharon could not. Dutifully, she nodded and listened to the information spouting forth. This building was new, that one had been renovated, and see where they had torn down all those ugly old tenements and put in condominiums? All very lovely, yes? But what of the poor souls who now had nowhere to live?

"And this building is very special to our family. We own it. Come, we will alight. You must see something in here." As soon as the car had stopped, she hopped out, not waiting for her uniformed driver to attend her, and dragged Sharon with her. A doorman bowed low and swung wide massive glass doors with gold lettering Sharon didn't have an opportunity to read, and then ushered them to an elevator on which he used a key and bowed again.

The doors whispered closed with expensive ease, enclosing them in carpeted, mirrored luxury. Though the ride was smooth and carried them high, it was soon over, and the doors opened again just as silently as they had closed.

"Where—" Are we, Sharon had been about to ask, staring around the beautifully appointed penthouse apartment.

A dainty hand closed over her mouth, and a

snapping dark eye winked at her. "Hush," Madame whispered. "I said I would not tell. I did not say I would not show. The rest, child, is up to you."

With that, she slipped back into the elevator.

From a room somewhere within the apartment, a tape played loudly. A golden oldie: "King of the Road." On shaking legs, Sharon followed the sound.

Marc lay on a wide leather couch, one long leg slung over the back, the other resting full length, his bare foot on the arm of the sofa. He was clean-shaven, his face craggy and worn looking, his eyes closed. With one hand he beat out the rhythm of the song on his bare abdomen just over the waistband of his jeans. His hair, she noted, was still too long.

The carpet underfoot was so thick, she could have walked across the room in army boots and he wouldn't have heard her, but she went quietly anyway, switched off the CD player, and stood there as his eyes popped open.

"All right, King of the Road," she said. "You seem to have come to rest."

Slowly, he swung his feet to the floor and sat up, never removing his gaze from her face. "I said I didn't want to see you," he told her. "Didn't you get the message?"

"I got it," she admitted. "But I didn't come all this way to hear that."

"So what did you come all dis way for?"

His slight slip in pronunciation told her more than anything that he wasn't as calm and unmoved as he pretended to be. She stepped toward him. As if to ward her off, or to gain the advantage of height, he got to his feet. She didn't stop until she was but inches from him. Tilting her head back, she looked at his stony face.

"I came to tell you that I love you. That I'm sorry for running, sorry for doubting you for even a little while. I came to ask your forgiveness, Marc."

He nodded, a tiny, tight movement. "I forgive you."

She widened her eyes in an attempt to keep the tears at bay. It was futile. "You don't sound very forgiving," she whispered, and blinked involuntarily, sending a curtain of shimmering drops down her face.

"Don't . . . please!" The words were dragged from him. He lifted a hand as if to touch her, and then let it fall, clenching his fists at his sides. A muscle in his shoulder jumped spasmodically. His face was deathly white.

"I'm sorry. I promised myself I wouldn't do that." With the back of her hand, she dried her face. "I can understand your anger, Marc. Or do I have to call you Jean-Marc now? I can understand it, truly, and I know I deserve it. I knew you better than to believe those old rumors. Only when it all happened, I didn't know you, and I believed them because of what was happening to me. So when I saw your name and realized that you weren't just Marc Duval, that you were that other man, the one I'd read about and thought such terrible things about, I was shocked and frightened and disillusioned. But only for a while, Marc! When I realized how wrong I'd been, I called you, but you didn't answer. It took me another hour to get home. By then, you were gone."

He nodded. "I had to leave. I've known it all along, Sharon. That's why I never asked you to marry me, because I knew it wouldn't work."

"Why wouldn't it work?" She lifted her gaze and her hand toward an ornately carved crucifix on one wall. "We never discussed it, I know. Are you a religious man?" she asked, a slow ache growing bigger and more bitter inside her. Had Ellis reached out of the past to destroy her present and her future? She had tried to make her marriage work! She had worked so hard at it, taken so much! Was she to be punished now because of things that had been no fault of hers? "Is it because I'm divorced?"

"No!" he said hoarsely. "Oh, Lord no, love! But Sharon, listen to me." He touched her then, his big hands closing over her shoulders, warm even through her coat. Over her collar, his thumbs stroked the sides of her neck. "I know how it would be, and I couldn't stand it. Each time we had an argument, each time I forgot myself and raised my voice, you'd be frightened, you'd remember the past and Ellis. And you'd think about the rumors about me, the taint on my character, and wonder. It would kill me to see doubt or fear in your eyes, Sharon. Please, it's better this way." With a gentle shove he set her back from him and let his hands fall to his sides again. "Don't make this any harder than it has to be. Just go."

She touched his bare chest with the tips of her fingers. "Marc, I can't go. Not without you. Please come home. Don't be mad at me any longer."

As if against his will, his hands flattened hers on his chest. His eyes burned into hers. "I'm not angry, Sharon. But I can't come back. It wouldn't work for us. Don't you see that?"

"No, dammit, I don't see that!" She snatched her hands free and wheeled away from him, turning at the other side of the room to face him, her dark eyes flaring with fury, fury he had never seen in her before. It startled him even as it fascinated him.

"I don't see that at all! But fine, if you don't

want to go back, I can come here! I can live anywhere, Marc, as long as you're there, too, and I
won't live without you!" She strode back to where
he stood and continued speaking, her voice getting louder and louder as she jabbed his chest
with a finger to make her points.

"Do you have any idea the agony I've been
through this past month, not knowing where you
were? Not knowing if you were alive or dead?"
This time, he got two fingers in the solar plexus.
"I advertised in all the papers, asking you to tell
me, just tell me if you were alive! I didn't even ask
you to see me or call me. A note would have done!
I've got a long-distance bill big enough to choke
an ox from calling your colleagues in Toronto, but
they wouldn't tell me anything! They claimed to
know nothing, but that was a lie, wasn't it? Just
another damned lie that men will tell for another
man in order to hold off a woman who wants to
find him. I hate the way men protect each other
from the consequences of their own actions! You
even told your father to say you didn't want to see
me! How do you justify that, Marc, making your
own father, a judge, for heaven's sake, lie for
you!"

"It wasn't a lie!" This time, he managed to capture her hand and hold it still. "I didn't want to
see you!"

"Oh, yes you did! If you hadn't wanted to see
me, if you hadn't wanted me to find you, you'd
have done what you did six years ago. You'd have
taken off again, running all over the world in
order to avoid me the way you did then to avoid
the pain. But no, you came here, home to your
family, where you knew I'd have to come and look
for you. Right, Marc? Right?"

She poked him with the index finger of the

other hand, and he snatched it into his control as well. "Wrong!" he thundered, dragging her tight against his chest, pinning her arms at her sides.

"Another lie!" she spat out, and her fury astounded him. He'd seen little fits of temper, tiny spurts of annoyance, but she had always backed down. He watched the dark of her eyes flare and dance with anger. She was not backing down now, that was obvious.

"Well, as you can see, it didn't work. Not your leaving, not your evasions, not your lies or your fine, masculine protective net! Because I stopped trying to get a man to help me and went to the best place of all, a woman! Your grandmother understands, dammit! She understands that I love you and you love me, and that should be enough at least to start building on!"

"Sharon—"

"You just shut up! I haven't finished what I came to say!" she said, wrenching free and grabbing him by the upper arms, trying to shake him. "You said you forgive me, but that's another lie! I hate lies, Marc! I hate them so much, I found it damned hard to forgive you for not telling from the very beginning who you are. But because I love you, I tried to understand, to put myself in your place and figure out why you held so much of yourself back. Okay, I know how hard it must have been for you, once you knew about my past, but you mistrusted me and my maturity for a hell of a lot longer than I mistrusted your integrity! I knew within an hour that I'd misjudged you! You've known me for months, and you're still misjudging me.

"Okay, fine. Maybe you're right. Maybe we don't belong together. But not because I'm afraid of you, Marc Duval, or ever will be. If we don't belong together, it's because you don't deserve me."

Suddenly, as if the anger had drained all her energy, she turned away, a long breath escaping her. "I've said what I had to say. Now, it's up to you. I know I can't force you. I'm staying at the Holiday Inn near the airport. You can call me there if—" Her voice broke and she struggled for control. Lifting her head, she made her way back to the paneled foyer. She stared at the dark brown wall, with its lighter wood strips every five feet, wondering dimly which one of them hid the elevator, and how she was supposed to call it.

"Open sesame?" she whispered.

"That won't do it," Marc said, turning her around.

"What will?"

He unbuttoned her coat, slid it off her shoulders, and let it slide to the floor. "This will," he said, his voice low, throbbing with feeling, as he slipped his hands into her hair and tilted her face up to his. He claimed her mouth in a deep kiss that left her knees weak and her head spinning.

After a moment, she said, "I don't see the elevator opening yet."

"Do you want it to?" She shook her head. "Then come back inside with me. There are things you have a right to know before you make a decision."

"I know all I need to know. I love you."

"And I love you, but that isn't enough. You deserve the truth, and until you have it from me, you're right, I don't deserve you."

Taking her hand, he led her back to the living room. Seating her on the couch, he paced away, looked out the window at a sky turned gray again. Hard, pebblelike snow began to beat on the glass.

"I loved Simone," he said. "But I was busy with a demanding career. I . . . neglected her. We argued about it. Often. We shouted at each other, often. She was a very volatile person. But we always made up." He turned and looked at her then, walking closer. "When she and Jean-Pierre were murdered, I was charged because one neighbor remembered those fights we'd had, and no one had noticed anything or anyone unusual in the neighborhood that day. It was known that I'd spent more nights at the office than I had at home in the previous year or so. Simone . . ." He swallowed and went on with difficulty. "Simone was nearly nine months pregnant when she was killed. There was talk that maybe I had done it because I'd learned the baby wasn't mine. It wasn't true. That child was mine. And I did not hit my wife, ever. I did not kill her and our baby and our son. This, I swear to you."

On trembling legs, she walked to where he stood and curled her hand around his taut jaw. "I know, my love. I know that."

He closed his eyes for a moment, then looked at her again, covering her hand with his, leaning his face into her palm as if seeking strength.

"Come and sit down with me, Marc . . . Jean-Marc."

"Marc," he whispered. "I'd rather you go on calling me that. It's . . . special. The 'Duval' is my mother's family name. I will stop using it now." He took her hand and went with her back to the sofa, sitting with his elbows on his knees, leaning forward, his fingers thrust into his hair.

"So many times I've wished the case had gone to a full trial—judge, jury, the works—and not been dismissed at the preliminary. Too many people had too many doubts, in spite of the fact that the judge berated the police for ever having laid the charges against me in the first place. 'Wasting the time of the court,' as he said, and 'besmirching the good name of an innocent man.' By that time, my good name was besmirched, and it was too late for apologies or explanations to make any difference."

Sharon rubbed the back of his neck as he talked, her fingers soothing tense muscles. "After the case was dismissed, I knew I couldn't function again as a prosecutor. I rejoined the family firm. We began to lose clients. I couldn't let that happen, so I quit. The rumors grew worse, more vicious. I could do nothing to change things except go away to ease the burden on my family."

He sat back and looked at her, his face haunted, his eyes full of shame. "I started to drink heavily. For weeks, I scarcely knew who I was or where I was, nor did I care. I didn't care about anything.

"My father found me one day in a filthy flophouse in Toronto. He dragged me out of there and sent me away to find his son; told me not to come back until I had."

She drew in a tremulous breath. "You found him, I guess. You came back."

"I found him, yes." Marc slid his hand over her sleek hair. "With your help, I found him, but I didn't bring him back with me. I left half of him on the other side of the country."

"Does your father know that?"

"Yes. He told me to go back. Back to you. To where I could be . . . complete."

"Good advice," she said, standing and walking away from him. When had his father told him that? A month ago when he first got home? "Are you going to take it?"

He stood, looking at her warily. "If you will forgive me, then I will."

She held out her arms and he came to her.

The next time she opened her eyes, Sharon found herself in a dimly lit bedroom, on her back on a bed, naked, with Marc leaning over her. "I love you," he said. "And you're right. I wasn't giving you any credit for maturity, for trusting me, for not likening me to you first husband."

"First?" she said. "I've only ever had the one."

"Not for long." He loved her with his eyes, his hands following the path his gaze seared along her body. Drawing his fingertips from her shoulder to her wrist, he encountered her gold bangles, riffled through them, hearing them jingle softly. "You wear these a lot. You were wearing them the first night I ever kissed you. They sounded like music when you put your arms around my neck. I just barely heard them over the pounding of my heart."

She smiled. Maybe someday she'd tell him. "The first time we kissed was the first time I'd ever kissed a man with a beard."

He rubbed his shaven skin. "My family was shocked. They said it wasn't me. How do you feel about it?"

"I like you better this way," she said without hesitation. "You have a strong chin. It seems a shame to hide it."

"I'm not hiding anything anymore," he said. "What you see is what you get."

She sat up and pushed him down onto his back, running her hands over his body, planting kisses here and there. "I like what I see. I love what I see. When do I get it?"

Catching her close in his arms, he rolled her

under him and crowded her legs apart with his own. "Now," he murmured. "Right now!"

A long time later, she smiled up at him and said, "You're incredible, Marc St.-Clair. You make the earth move."

"Uh-uh." He shook his shaggy head deprecatingly. "Not that incredible. Maybe I made the earth move, but I don't think I made the elevator door open yet."

She laughed, remembering that he had claimed a kiss would do it. "Tsk!" She shook her head. "I guess we're trapped in here, then?"

"I guess so. At least until we figure out what it's going to take."

Snuggling closer, she said, "Maybe it's just going to take time."

"Right," he murmured. "Let's take our time, sweetheart. All the time in the world."

Epilogue

Sharon lay in bed, propped on one elbow, watching her husband sleep. The birds outside had begun their dawn chorus an hour before, waking her long before the sun was up. Now, as always, she heard music in the song of the birds as they greeted the fresh June morning, music she knew she'd be writing before the day was out.

She cherished these moments in early morning, before Marc and the children were awake. They were her moments, time to reflect on the joys of her life, time to dream of the pleasures of the future, time to cradle with a loving hand the new life that was growing within her, not yet evident except to her. She thought that today she would tell Marc, so that he could rejoice with her. She needed no doctor to confirm what she knew was true.

She had so much. There could be no greater happiness than this, she though. Beside her, making her jump, the telephone rang, loud in the slumberous room. Quickly, she lifted it, but not before Marc came fully awake, his eyes wide with concern as he gazed at her.

He saw her smile and relaxed as she said, "Hello, Papa. It's good to hear your voice. No, no of course it's not too early for me. I was awake. No, please don't worry about the three-hour time difference. It doesn't matter that you forgot. Do you want to talk to Jean-Marc?"

She laughed at the reply, and delightful color tinged her cheeks. A moment later she handed Marc the phone and lay back against her pillow, twisting the cord in her fingers as she watched his face while he spoke to his father, scolding him for having flirted with his wife and made her blush.

Then, his smile faded. A frown appeared between his brows. His chiseled mouth took on a taut, hard appearance. Sharon took his free hand in her own. His fingers curled tensely around it. He listened, spoke quietly a few times, and then handed her the phone to hang up.

"What is it, love?" she asked, hitching herself back up on her elbow. "Marc? It's not bad news, is it?" His father hadn't sounded tense or strained. There had been no warning of anything dreadful.

"Marc?"

He drew her down against his chest and ran a hand into her hair. She felt his fingers trembling. "No," he said. "Not bad news. But, I guess, disturbing."

"Can you talk about it?"

He rolled her onto her back and leaned up over her. "With you? Of course. With you, I can talk of anything." But she could see that it wasn't easy for him.

"It was about Simone and Jean-Pierre," he said.

"About their murder. Papa says it will be in the papers today."

"He . . . he's been caught?"

Marc nodded. "The police were investigating a different crime and found some evidence in a house. Things taken from my home that link two brothers with the crime. They confessed as soon as they were confronted. They were . . . they were members of a satanic cult when they killed Simone and Jean-Pierre."

"Oh, Marc!" She remembered the rumors to that effect, all those years ago. She curled her hand around the back of his neck as his face creased with pain and tears flooded his eyes. He dropped his head to her shoulder. For long moments, she held him while he relived some of the grief of years before. "I'm sorry," he said presently, lifting his head.

With the corner of the sheet, she tenderly wiped his damp face. "No, my darling, you must never be sorry for those feelings. They are part of you, part of what makes you the man I love. You loved your family, Marc. You have a right to your sorrow."

"I know, and all this time I expected to hate the man who killed them, but now that I know he— they've—been caught, I find I don't. I pity them. Part of my sorrow is for them, for what they've been through and still have to go through," he said, shocking her. "And for their family."

"What? How can you care about them after what they did?" The boys' parents, she could understand pitying. But the murderers? Never! What kind of pity have they shown?

"Neither my hating them nor even their remorse can bring back the dead. And it seems they do have remorse. They've had to live with what they did for a long time."

Sharon sat up quickly. "Well, if you're not angry with them, I'm furious on your behalf! What right did they have to destroy the lives of those you loved, and your life, too, at the same time?"

"No right, of course. And I am angry, *chérie*, but more angry about the terrible lack of reason behind a crime like that. They had nothing to gain. Their motive wasn't even robbery. And they are so young. In their early twenties. They were mere children."

They both fell silent, holding each other. How she loved him! Sharon thought. Even when he should have been railing against the murderers, seeking revenge, he was concerned with their well-being, seeing their side of it. The court system needed people like him, caring, judicious people who were capable of empathy.

"Marc?" she said after several minutes had passed. "It's over now, love. You can go back, back to practicing law without ever having to worry again about what people think."

He lifted his head, touched her face, smiled. "Yes. It's over now, angel. And you're right. I can go back to the law. I think I likely will. But oddly, since I met you, my worry hasn't been what other people thought, only what you thought. I was sure I had buried the past before, but I was wrong. This has been preying on me. Always, I have wondered if you truly believed me incapable of harming my family. My past one or my present one."

"I have never believed you capable of that," she said, taking his hand and sliding it under the covers, laying it low on her abdomen, pressing it to the small hard mass she had felt there this past week. "If I had thought there was danger, would I have wanted this?"

He tilted his head to one side, cocking a brow. "Wanted what?" He knew what she *wasn't* talking about. She didn't have that look in her eyes. Not quite.

She smiled a sweet and secret smile. "Your—our—future family."

His breath left him suddenly as he understood, and he cupped his hand over her abdomen. His eyes glazed over and he buried his face in her hair. "Our baby?" he said when he could talk. "Are you sure?" His voice was ragged, but his face was suffused with joy.

She laughed at him, wrapping her arms around his neck, nestling her body against his. "Our baby. I'm as sure as I've ever been about something like this. But if you want to make absolutely certain . . . ?"

Now that look was in her eyes! He smothered their shared laughter with a kiss, and took her up on her offer. It never hurt to make doubly sure.

THE EDITOR'S CORNER

As you look forward to the holiday season—the most romantic season of all—you can plan on enjoying some of the very best love stories of the year from LOVESWEPT. Our authors know that not all gifts come in boxes wrapped in pretty paper and tied with bows. In fact, the most special gifts are the gifts that come from the heart, and in each of the six LOVESWEPTs next month, characters are presented with unique gifts that transform their lives through love.

Whenever we publish an Iris Johansen love story, it's an event! In **AN UNEXPECTED SONG,** LOVESWEPT #438, Iris's hero, Jason Hayes, is mesmerized by the lovely voice of singer Daisy Justine and realizes instantly that she was born to sing his music. But Daisy has obligations that mean more to her than fame and fortune. She desperately wants the role he offers, but even more she wants to be touched, devoured by the tormented man who tangled his fingers in her hair. Jason bestows upon Daisy the gift of music from his soul, and in turn she vows to capture his heart and free him from the darkness where he's lived for so long. This hauntingly beautiful story is a true treat for all lovers of romance from one of the genre's premier authors.

In **SATURDAY MORNINGS,** LOVESWEPT #439, Peggy Webb deals with a different kind of gift, the gift of belonging. To all observers, heroine Margaret Leigh Jones is a proper, straitlaced librarian who seems content with her life—until she meets outrageous rogue Andrew McGill when she brings him her poodle to train. Then she wishes she knew how to flirt instead of how to blush! And Andrew's

(continued)

peaceful Saturday mornings are never the same after Margaret Leigh learns a shocking family secret that sends her out looking for trouble and for ways to hone her womanly wiles. All of Andrew's possessive, protective instincts rush to the fore as he falls head over heels for this crazy, vulnerable woman who tries just a bit too hard to be brazen. Through Andrew's love Margaret Leigh finally sees the error of her ways and finds the answer to the questions of who she really is and where she belongs—as Andrew's soul mate, sharing his Saturday mornings forever.

Wonderful storyteller Lori Copeland returns next month with another lighthearted romp, 'TIZ THE SEASON, LOVESWEPT #440. Hero Cody Benderman has a tough job ahead of him in convincing Darby Piper that it's time for her to fall in love. The serious spitfire of an attorney won't budge an inch at first, when the undeniably tall, dark, and handsome construction foreman attempts to turn her orderly life into chaos by wrestling with her in the snow, tickling her breathless beside a crackling fire—and erecting a giant holiday display that has Darby's clients up in arms. But Darby gradually succumbs to Cody's charm, and she realizes he's given her a true gift of love—the gift of discovering the simple joys in life and taking the time to appreciate them. She knows she'll never stop loving or appreciating Cody!

LOVESWEPT #441 by Terry Lawrence is a sensuously charged story of UNFINISHED PASSION. Marcie Courville and Ray Crane meet again as jurors on the same case, but much has changed in the ten years since the ruggedly sexy construction worker had awakened the desire of the pretty, privi-

(continued)

leged young woman. In the intimate quarters of the jury room, each feels the sparks that still crackle between them, and each reacts differently. Ray knows he can still make Marcie burn with desire—and now he has so much more to offer her. Marcie knows she made the biggest mistake of her life when she broke Ray's heart all those years ago. But how can she erase the past? Through his love for her, Ray is able to give Marcie a precious gift—the gift of rectifying the past—and Marcie is able to restore the pride of the first man she ever loved, the only man she ever loved. Rest assured there's no unfinished passion between these two when the happy ending comes!

Gail Douglas makes a universal dream come true in **IT HAD TO BE YOU,** LOVESWEPT #442. Haven't you ever dreamed of falling in love aboard a luxury cruise ship? I can't think of a more romantic setting than the *QE2.* For Mike Harris it's love at first sight when he spots beautiful nymph Caitlin Grant on the dock. With her endless legs and sea-green eyes, Caitlin is his male fantasy come true—and he intends to make the most of their week together at sea. For Caitlin the gorgeous stranger in the Armani suit seems to be a perfect candidate for a shipboard romance. But how can she ever hope for more with a successful doctor who will never be able to understand her wanderer's spirit and the joy she derives from taking life as it comes? Caitlin believes she is following her heart's desire by traveling and experiencing life to the fullest—until her love for Mike makes her realize her true desire. He gives her restless heart the gift of a permanent home in his arms—and she promises to stay forever.

(continued)

Come along for the ride as psychologist Maya Stephens draws Wick McCall under her spell in **DEEPER AND DEEPER**, LOVESWEPT #443, by Jan Hudson. The sultry-eyed enchantress who conducts the no-smoking seminar has a voice that pours over Wick like warm honey, but the daredevil adventurer can't convince the teacher to date a younger man. Maya spends her days helping others overcome their problems, but she harbors secret terrors of her own. When Wick challenges her to surrender to the wildness beneath the cool facade she presents to the world, she does, reveling in his sizzling caresses and drowning in the depths of his tawny-gold eyes. For the first time in her life Maya is able to truly give of herself to another—not as a teacher to a student, but as a woman to a man, a lover to her partner—and she has Wick to thank for that. He's shown her it's possible to love and not lose, and to give everything she has and not feel empty inside, only fulfilled.

Enjoy next month's selection of LOVESWEPTs, while you contemplate what special gifts from the heart you'll present to those you love this season!

Sincerely,

Susann Brailey

Susann Brailey
Editor
LOVESWEPT
Bantam Books
666 Fifth Avenue
New York, NY 10103

FOREVER LOVESWEPT

SPECIAL KEEPSAKE
EDITION OFFER
$12⁹⁵
VALUE

Here's your chance to receive a special hardcover Loveswept "Keepsake Edition" to keep close to your heart forever. Collect hearts (shown on next page) found in the back of Loveswepts #426-#449 (on sale from September 1990 through December 1990). Once you have collected a total of 15 hearts, fill out the coupon and selection form on the next page (no photocopies or hand drawn facsimiles will be accepted) and mail to: Loveswept Keepsake, P.O. Box 9014, Bohemia, NY 11716.

FOREVER LOVESWEPT
SPECIAL KEEPSAKE EDITION OFFER
SELECTION FORM

Choose from these special Loveswepts by your
favorite authors. Please write a 1 next to your first
choice, a 2 next to your second choice. Loveswept
will honor your preference as inventory allows.

Loveswept®

_____BAD FOR EACH OTHER   Billie Green

_____NOTORIOUS   Iris Johansen

_____WILD CHILD   Suzanne Forster

_____A WHOLE NEW LIGHT   Sandra Brown

_____HOT TOUCH   Deborah Smith

_____ONCE UPON A TIME...GOLDEN
        THREADS   Kay Hooper

Attached are 15 hearts and the selection form which
indicates my choices for my special hardcover Loveswept
"Keepsake Edition." Please mail my book to:

NAME:_____

ADDRESS:_____

CITY/STATE:_____ZIP:_____

Offer open only to residents of the United States, Puerto Rico and
Canada. Void where prohibited, taxed, or restricted. Allow 6 - 8
weeks after receipt of coupons for delivery. Offer expires
January 15, 1991. You will receive your first choice as inventory
allows; if that book is no longer available, you'll receive your
second choice, etc.

THE SHAMROCK TRINITY

☐ **21975 RAFE, THE MAVERICK**
by Kay Hooper $2.95

☐ **21976 YORK, THE RENEGADE**
by Iris Johansen $2.95

☐ **21977 BURKE, THE KINGPIN**
by Fayrene Preston $2.95